HRYHORIY KVITKA·OSNOVYANENKO

the WITCH *of* KONOTOP

UKRAINIAN BOOK INSTITUTE

This book has been published with the support of the Translate Ukraine Translation Program

THE WITCH OF KONOTOP

by Hryhoriy Kvitka-Osnovyanenko

First published in Ukrainian as *Конотопська відьма* in 1836

Translated from the Ukrainian
by Michael M. Naydan and Alla Perminova

**This book has been published with the support
of the Translate Ukraine Translation Program**

Edited by Ludmilla A. Trigos

www.glagoslav.com

ISBN: 978-1-80484-116-7
ISBN: 978-1-80484-117-4

First published in English by Glagoslav Publications in November 2023

A catalogue record for this book is available from the British Library.

Hryhoriy Kvitka-Osnovyanenko

the Witch *of* Konotop

TRANSLATED FROM THE UKRAINIAN
BY MICHAEL M. NAYDAN AND ALLA PERMINOVA

GLAGOSLAV PUBLICATIONS

HRYHORIY KVITKA-OSNOVYANENKO

(1778–1843)

CONTENTS

Dedicated to the bright memory of Bohdan Zholdak,

who penned theatrical and filmscript versions of

The Witch of Konotop.

*He was a great friend, whose boundless good heart, marvelous
wit, and effervescent charm will never be forgotten
by all of us touched by his life.*

ACKNOWLEDGEMENTS

We are extremely grateful to folklorist Natalie Kononen-ko for providing her expert commentary on Ukrainian folk beliefs in her guest introduction to this volume as well as to Max Mendor for his outstanding efforts on the cover design. Great thanks also to our editor Ludmilla A. Trigos for her expert emendations to our translation.

A BIOGRAPHICAL NOTE

Michael M. Naydan

Hryhoriy Kvitka-Osnovyanenko (1778–1843) is considered "the father of Ukrainian prose." In the writer's time it was common to take a hyphenated name when both surnames of the parents of an individual were from prominent families – thus the hyphenation in his name. He was born to a well-to-do gentry family in 1778 in the settlement of Osnova, which then was on the outskirts of the city of Kharkiv. He grew up at a time when Ukraine had been colonized by the Russian empire. He received his early education through home schooling and later continued his studies at a monastery school. He particularly developed a love for art, literature, and music in his studies and was a proficient pianist. From 1793 to 1797 he served in the military as was common at the time and as a public servant. He retired at the rank of captain. When he was 26, he entered the Kuriazh Orthodox Monastery but left it after serving as a novice for ten months. As a result of his upbringing and faith, one finds a deep layer of religiosity and a moral tonality underpinning much of his writing.

Kvitka-Osnovyanenko became a tireless cultural activist for his indigenous Ukrainian people and grew up bilingual. Besides native fluency in Ukrainian, he was also fluent in Russian, the language of the empire. Thus, he was able to navigate between the two languages to create a space for Ukrainian among the dominant colonizing Russian culture.

He helped establish the Kharkiv Theater in 1812 and served as its first director. He founded the Ukrainian journal *The Ukrainian Messenger* in Kharkiv as well as the almanacs *Morning Star* and *Fresh Ice*, which all promoted Ukrainian authors on their pages. He also served in several civic positions including county marshal of the nobility (1816–1828) as well as president of the Kharkiv criminal court after that. He devoted much of his life to civic causes: helping indigent children and establishing an institute for girls. He also held the position of curator of the first public library in Kharkiv.

As a writer, Kvitka-Osnovyanenko was a late bloomer. He began his literary career first writing in Russian in 1820 and then later focused on Ukrainian. His volume *Little Russian Anecdotes* was published in 1822 when he was 44 years old. "Little Russia" or "Russia Minor" was a colonial appellation that Russians used for Ukraine in the eighteenth and nineteenth centuries. His first Ukrainian-language short story "The Portrait of a Soldier: A Latin Tall Tale as Told in Our Language" appeared in 1833. In 1836 he published his classic *The Witch of Konotop*, which contains elements of satire as well as indigenous Ukrainian folklore. Comedy has been one of the genres used by colonized minorities to create a space for their own language and culture. In this way colonized peoples often present their own culture as non-threating, making them acceptable for the majority colonizing language and culture. This is the way that Ukrainian writer Ivan Kotlyarevsky portrayed his drunken Ukrainian Kozaks (aka Cossacks) in his mock epic based on Virgil's *The Aeneid – Eneida* (1799) as a travesty, which was exotic and entertaining for the Russian reading public of the time. However, the work served a dual purpose: it codified the vernacular Ukrainian language in print and in part became the basis for the modern Ukrainian literary language. Kvitka-Osnovyanenko continued in that vein of Kotlyarevsky. While comedy was his genre of choice in his early Ukrainian writings, he later proved in his prose that the Ukrainian language was suitable for serious topics.

Critics have divided Kvitka-Osnovyanenko's creative work essentially into two categories: comical burlesque writings and sentimental realistic works that describe village life in Ukraine in ethnographic detail. Women often appear as the heroes of his prose. His satirical Russian-language drama *A Visitor from the Capital or Turmoil in a District Town* (1827) may have influenced Myhola Hohol's (aka Nikolai Gogol) play *The Inspector General* (1835).[1] While Hohol and Kvitka-Osnovyanenko knew each other, Hohol denied any influence of the latter's writing. Kvitka-Osnovyanenko's Russian-language novella *Elections of the Gentry* (1828) resonated with the reading public in Moscow but was banned by Tsar Nicholas I after he read it. His Ukrainian-language novella *Marusya* (1832) marked a high point in the development of his sentimental prose, which presented moving portraits of his characters meant to elicit empathy from readers. He published Volume I of his *Little Russian Tales as Told by Hrytsko Osnovyanenko* in 1834 and Volume II in 1836–7. The lengthy short story "Tumbleweed," which is included in our translation here, appeared among those tales. Many Russians have long and wrongly argued that Ukrainian is a dialect of Russian unworthy of separate status as a literary language. Two centuries of myriad prominent Ukrainian writers obviously refutes that idiotic claim. In the Ukrainian literary tradition Kvitka-Osnovyanenko is also well known as a playwright for his comedies *Shelmenko the District Scribe* (1831), *Matchmaking at Honcharivka* (1834), and *Shelmenko the Orderly* (1837). He is remembered as one of the most prominent makers and promoters of Ukrainian culture in the early nineteenth-century.

---

[1] See Viktoriia Lebovich's article "*Priiezhii iz stolitsty, ili Sumatokha v uezdnom gorode i Revizor*," in *Studia Slavica*, 63/1 (2018), pp. 89–96.

A NOTE ON THE TRANSLATION

Michael M. Naydan

The Witch of Konotop is a comedic nineteenth-century classic that has become part of the Ukrainian literary canon virtually since its publication in 1836. It was written in 1833. It has not previously been available in English for reasons that we as translators now better understand after tackling it. The essential hurdle for the translator consists of the novel's complicated vocabulary and linguistic structures as well as its stylistic levels that range from archaic Old Church Slavonicisms in the company scribe Pistrak's speech patterns to the colorful, colloquial language of Kozak Captain Zabryokha, who has great difficulty in understanding what his underling and colleague often is saying. This confusion of mismatched tongues that leads to conflict comprises much of the humor in the first half of the novel. How does one convey that archaic style of a bookish language that is meant only to be written and used primarily in religious services and religious contexts? We have opted for pseudo-Elizabethan English in this translation as well as some King James Biblical locutions to try to convey some of the effect of the scribe's speech patterns in English. The two main characters speak in diametrically different voices, so we try our best to get across some of that texture, which at times is more important than pure linguistic accuracy.

Kvitka-Osnovyanenko's style, too, presents a precursor to Mykola Hohol's in the latter's Russian-language works. The folksy beginning of *The Witch of Konotop* recalls aspects of Rudy Panko's opening narration found in Hohol's *Evenings on a Farm near Dikanka* (written 1829–1832 and published in 1833). Kvitka-Osnovyanenko makes use of Hohol-like insignificant detail and ironic asides in *The Witch of Konotop*, whose comedic approach echoes that of Hohol's in the latter's works such as *The Inspector General*, "The Overcoat," and "The Nose." The theme of the supernatural in terms of the folk belief in witches and demons also links Kvitka-Osnovyanenko's *The Witch of Konotop* with Hohol's early Ukrainian-themed works, which contain numerous witches and demons and largely rely on indigenous Ukrainian folk beliefs, which Hohol acquired in letters from his mother. The theme of acquisition and desire leading one to ruin also links Kvitka's writings with Hohol's in the latter's short stories such as "The Tale of how Ivan Ivanovich and Ivan Nikiforovich Squabbled" and "The Overcoat," as well as in the novel *Dead Souls*.

We have translated one other of Kvitka-Osnovyanenko's novellas for this volume to feature the more serious side of his writing. The story "Tumbleweed" exhibits ethnographic detail of Ukrainian village life in the early part of the nineteenth century with a didactic, moralistic tale about a senseless crime committed with the uncovering of the crime's perpetrator by a tumbleweed rolling in the wind that identifies him as though it had been directed by the hand of God. Kvitka-Osnovyanenko exhibits elements of psychologism in his story with an overriding sentimental pathos. Even the tumbleweed itself suggests supernatural forces at work because born witches who are bound to do good in the Ukrainian folk tradition can appear in the form of tumbleweed. I'm grateful to Natalie Kononenko pointing that out to me. While Ukrainian peasants in the story suffer from poverty, their honesty, dignity, hard work, and faith lead them to higher truths.

These early classics of Ukrainian literature deserve to find a readership in the Western world. We are glad to play a role in bringing them to you in this volume.

WITCHCRAFT BELIEFS IN
THE WITCH OF KONOTOP

Natalie Kononenko

Hryhory Kvitka-Osnovyanenko's *The Witch of Konotop* does not fully follow folk beliefs about witches. It does, however, present a widely held Ukrainian belief. That belief is as current now as it was at the time that our author wrote his text. In just about every area of Ukraine, in just about every stratum of society, people believe that one should not strive to possess that which belongs to someone else. It is perfectly fine and desirable to try and better one's self and one's lot in life. But, if advancement is at a cost to another person, if achieving a certain position means depriving another of that position, that is not acceptable. If winning a lover means taking her or him away from another person, that is to be condemned. The scribe Prokip Ryhorovych Pistryak seeks to discredit our hero, Captain Mykyta Ulasovych Zabryokha, hoping to disqualify him from holding his position as captain of the Konotop forces. He tries to show that Captain Mykyta is incompetent, a situation that should lead to his removal and thus open the path for Prokip to assume his job. This, both in terms of our text and according to current social norms, is a gross violation of proper behavior. When Captain Mykyta courts the beautiful Olena, he is acting in a perfectly acceptable manner. But when she rejects him, and even more when he learns that she loves another and he seeks to magically separate the lovers and win Olena for himself, then he too is violating social norms and committing an immoral act.

But how do witches figure into this social dynamic? In Kvitka-Osnovyanenko narrative, the scheming Prokip tries to discredit Captain Mykyta by convincing him to conduct a witch hunt. Mykyta and his fighting men of Konotop have been summoned to Chernihiv, but Prokip convinces the captain that they cannot go because there is more immediate threat at home that must be removed. Specifically, he says that witches are controlling the weather and preventing rain. Mykyta must discover the local witch and thus restore climate normalcy. Prokip assumes that, if Mykyta goes along with his scheme, his belief in witches will show him to be ignorant and backwards and unworthy of his rank as captain. This, the scribe posits, will clear the way for Prokip to assume his position. Prokip proposes a public test that will lead to the discovery of the local witch. The method of determining who is and who is not a witch is something that was actually practiced in Ukraine, namely the "swimming of witches." This requires the dunking of suspected women. Those who drown as a result are considered to be normal human beings. Those who do not drown are suspected of witchcraft. When this procedure is conducted, in Kvitka-Osnovyanenko's narrative, most of the suspects, who are, as one might expect, female and elderly, drown. But one woman, Yavdokha Zubykha, does not drown no matter how often and in what manner she is dunked. All realize that she is, indeed, a witch.

In the narrative here, Zubykha's extraordinary powers are explained by saying that she is a born witch. In Ukrainian folk tradition, there is a distinction between born and learned witches. Born witches come by their power naturally. They may be born with a special mark on the body such as a caul, a piece of the placenta on top on the baby's head. A born witch may be the seventh daughter of seven daughters or the seventh son of seven sons. Closely connected to born witches are people who have a near-death experience. These people, having been to the spirit world and back, can reenter that world as needed. All of these people do not seek their supernatural ability; they come by it through life circumstances. They are contrasted to learned witches. These are people who actively seek supernatural power. To gain it, they typically perform a sacrilegious act such as stabbing an icon with a knife or stomping on it.

The contrast between born and learned witches characterizes not only the means by which they obtain supernatural power, but also the way in which their abilities are exercised. Born witches are healers. They help people. They treat colicky babies and calm frightened children. They sooth the pain of burns. They aid the sick of all ages. And they do so to be helpful. They do not seek financial compensation or any other reward. Learned witches are believed to have acquired their power for personal gain. This gain is usually financial. They are said to sell their services. They are believed to have the ability to steal milk from the cows of their neighbors, thus prospering in an unnatural and inexplicable manner. Born witches are sought as helpers; learned witches, if their identity is known, are people to avoid unless one is desperate enough to purchase their services. The term "witch," or v*id'ma*, is typically not used for born witches: it is reserved for learned witches. Born masters of the supernatural are referred to as *baba*, the word for grandmother. They can have an adjective appended to their name such as *baba povitukha*, a woman who helps with babies, or *baba kostoprav*, a woman who sets bones.

Of course, things are never simple and born witches may be suspected of malefice. Born witches can have power that is startling, and this may cause people to fear them. During one of my trips to Ukraine, my husband came with me and made the mistake of carrying the backpack with my photographic and recording equipment on just one shoulder. He dislocated a disk in his spine and was in terrible pain. We were attending a conference in Odesa at the time and were housed at a naval facility. We sought the help of the resident nurse, and she proved to be most caring and kind, giving my husband painkilling injections and a spinal support belt. This provided relief but did not solve his problem. From Odesa, we traveled to a village where had I planned to work. There, upon the advice of my cousin, I sought the help of one of the resident healers. She performed a massage and essentially realigned my husband's spine. When something miraculous occurs, such as having a village woman solve a problem that a medically trained specialist cannot fix, then special forces can seem to be at work. The woman who provides the solution to a terrible problem may indeed seem to be possessed of supernatural power. Once the specialness of an individual has been established, she is set apart from the rest of the social group. When anything out of the ordinary occurs, bad things as well as good, then thoughts of the special individual come to the fore. Thus, when one's cow stops giving milk or gives less milk than before, a woman of power might be suspected of syphoning off some of that milk for her own benefit, especially if her own household does not suffer from lack of milk. The motif of Zubykha procuring milk from animals by supernatural means does occur in Kvitka-Osnovyanenko's narrative and this is likely a reference to this folk belief. In essence, a special individual is suspected of being special in all respects and capable of doing harm as well as good. When a person refuses a woman something that she has requested and then suffers an illness in the family, such a woman might be suspected of exacting revenge. This is indeed what happened (and sometimes still happens) in villages and perhaps in urban settings as well. In such cases, even someone who was considered a healer can be reclassified as a *vid'ma*, a witch.

Captain Mykyta turns to Zubykha for help with his love life, and she does interfere in the life of Olena, the woman the Captain desires. Whether women like Zubykha were actually able to redirect desire from one person to another is questionable, but the belief that this was indeed something that they could do was widespread. Kateryna Dysa's book[2] about witchcraft trials in Ukraine does provide ample evidence of people turning to women who were believed to possess supernatural powers to either secure the love of someone who was indifferent to the person seeking help or to direct away the love of someone whose attention was not desired. Whether *baby* (the plural of *baba*) or *vid'my* (the plural of *vid'ma* or witch) actually practiced love magic is not clear. Certainly, they were accused of such practices when something unusual or unexpected happened, as Dysa's book attests.

In Kvitka-Osnovyanenko's text, all of the protagonists suffer for their actions. It is not clear whether the misfortune that comes their way is caused by their desire for something that belonged to another. The role that witchcraft played in their downfall is ambiguous. None of the major figures in the narrative live happily ever after, however. Zubykha, the witch of Konotop, suffers the most. She lies on her deathbed, but cannot die, and is condemned to extended and gruesome mortal agony. It is only when people break a hole in the roof over her head and a mysterious force or entity is released that she finds death and peace. Creating a hole in the roof above the deathbed of a witch is a motif that exists in folk belief. And it applies to learned witches only, not born ones. Those who are born witches die peacefully. They never took something that was not theirs and have nothing to surrender. Learned witches acquired something that was not natural, a power that they were not destined to possess. It is they who

....

[2] Katheryn Dysa, *Ukrainian Witchcraft Trials: Volhynia, Podolia, and Ruthenia, 17th–18th Centuries.* Budapest – New York: Central European University Press, 2020.

must give up that illegitimately acquired thing in order to die in peace.

Hryhory Kvitka-Osnovyanenko's text does not accurately reproduce Ukrainian folk belief about witches but references the complex of witchcraft beliefs and practices to a sufficient extent to produce a moving and effective narrative.

THE WITCH
OF KONOTOP

I

The sad and unhappy Kozak Captain Mykyta Ulasovych Zabryokha[3] was sitting on a bench in a new attic loft that was separated from the rest of his house on the other side of his inside porch. Although the lad was usually tidy, he wasn't wearing a white shirt this holy Sunday and – forgive us for this expression – he hadn't taken off his blue nankeen trousers for the night. Yes, poor guy, he had slept in them, so very happy that he had made his way home by midnight; and right then and there, whether he had fallen asleep or not, he was awakened even before sunrise. He jumped up right away, yawned, scratched himself, prayed to God, sniffed some strong snuff three times, listened to what they were reading to him, gave some orders, and, remaining alone in the room, plopped himself down on the bench. His hair was disheveled, his scalp lock untrimmed, his kisser unwashed, his eyes sleepy, his whiskers uncurled, and his shirt loose. Lying at the edge of the table were his pipe and wallet, an

. . . .

[3] Ukrainians among other Eastern Slavic peoples have a tradition of using the patronymic as a sign of respect. Ulasovych would mean the son of Ulas. In Ukrainian "sotnyk" would technically be the rank of a lieutenant, who would be in charge of a Kozak "sotnya" or hundred-man company. We've rendered the rank here as "captain" in English to indicate the commensurate level of his military responsibility and translated the word "sotnya" as "company." Last names can be quite meaningful and often humorous in Ukrainian, and the captain's last name Zabryokha means a bespattered person.

inkwell, a comb, and a tankard filled with last-year's infused pear liqueur, which Pazka had poured into a bottle for him last evening. But although he had poured it into the tankard, in order, you know, to drink out of sorrow, since he started to fret again, he forgot about it, lay down, and fell asleep. And now, having grown tired, he didn't really hurry back to that tankard, for a new misfortune had completely twisted him up, though he himself didn't understand the cause of his fretting. What misfortune befell him, and why did such sorrow overwhelm him? Well! Be patient, and I'll tell you the whole story: from whence he arrived home so late, and why he had such a bad night's sleep. Here, look, just take a little bit of the stronger snuff, and listen.

Pan[4] Captain Ulasovych was from an honest, noteworthy lineage. Since time immemorial, after all, a hundred officers were all Zabryokhas; and Mykyta's grandfathers and great-grandfathers were Captains in the glorious little town of Captains Konotop. Thus, from father to son the hundredth one came in succession after the previous ones. Just when old Ulas Zabryokha, a Captain of Konotop, had died... oh how the Kozaks regretted his passing! And the people, both old and young, all wept. And at his funeral, his coffin was carried through the entire village in the people's arms, the way a father carries his child. They interred him near the church and commemorated him well at many funeral repasts. When they marked the fortieth day of his passing with raised toasts, when the people gathered to give advice about whom should be designated Captain, they all spoke in a single voice and

____

[4] "Pan" means "Mr." in Ukrainian and is a common polite form of address. It can be used with a person's first or last name as well as with a person's profession or, in the case of this text, with one's father's profession. The forms "Pani" (Mrs.) and "Panna" (Miss) are used in the same way. We've used the Ukrainian forms of the word to maintain the flavor of the text and to avoid awkwardness in English.

shouted out: "Who should it be? Ulas Zabryokha's son; who else better could we find?"

And Zabryokha was designated Captain. From a Zabryoshchenko,[5] he became just Zabryokha. Then after burying his father, he looked around, and he was already – give or take – twenty-five. You can't get around it, time to get married, time to go lookin' for a gal... For his father, old Ulas, had been on the stingy side, and when it happened that Mykyta had gone to him for a heart-to-heart talk and started to ask his father to marry him off, the old man would furrow his brow, stand up and look at him, and say: "Let the weather just clear up, look, it's gotten cloudy. What kind of half-decent son is getting married now? Look, grain's expensive, five altyns[6] for a sack. And it will be cramped for us if we takes on a wife for you: we just have this house with a room, and across the inner porch there's another house, and that's it. Where could I fit you and the kids, I already knows that you'll have tons of them. Let's just think about it later." Mykyta would just scratch himself and leave after that refusal. Now that the old man had died, he was free to do as he pleased. Having taken the adjacent house, now he built a wall, and he had an additional spacious upper room there. Then he began to look for a girl and sat down to think. Who had he not thought about already? Moreover, where from? Now he set his eyes on the Chernihiv archpriest's daughter and was scared off by the gap in status: you wouldn't be able to fit all her clothes on two carts, and, her father, they says, will toss necklaces in bundles, and that's nothin'. The seminarians ate pig slop baked pumpkins there, so our lad had no good rea-

[5] A little Zabryokha or son of Zabryokha. The -enko suffix is typical of Ukrainian Kozak last names. For example, the name Honcharenko would be "little Honchar" (potter) or "son of the potter."

[6] An altyn was a three-kopeck coin that was used as currency in eighteenth-century Ukraine and in the Russian empire.

son to hurry over. So, he decided to set the bar lower, kept mulling things over and over, he thought some and kept on thinking... then he slapped his palms together and shouted out to himself in the house: "Aha! She's mine! Laddie! Saddle the horse as quick as you can!" Whether he was ready or not, our Ulasovych mounted his horse oh so quick... and once he started his giddyap, he was long gone in no time.

Where did he head off so swiftly? Eh! Once, somewhere at a fair, he had seen the Kozak calvary cornet's[7] daughter Olena, over there at a farmstead on Sukha Balka [Dry Gully], nicknamed Bezverkhy Khutir [Hilless Farmstead]. While looking the girl over, he was really surprised that she was so young, but still bought a lot of flour; and as he began to ask people about her, he was told that she didn't have a father or mother, but just a brother; that she was a diligent homemaker, whether she tended the cows, or worked in the field with mowers and reapers, and in winter she took care of things herself in the brewery and prepared all the grain for it. Her brother, the cornet's son, though a young man, didn't want to get married, but was thinking about becoming a monk, because when he was sick, he made himself a promise: "When," he said, "I get better, I'll become a monk, after giving away my sister in marriage." So, he recovered and waited for a good man to come around to give him both control of the household and his sister, and he cared about nothing else, just reading books, and Olena took care of everything in the household for him.

Our Pan Captain Zabryokha was drawn there. It was not like he had to use a hell of a lot of imagination! The cat knows where they keep the pig lard: not only is that

....

[7] "Korundzhyi" in Ukrainian means the "standard-bearer." We've opted for the British military term "cornet" that has the same meaning. "Khorundzhivna" in this context would be the cornet's daughter. It could also mean a cornet's wife in other contexts.

girl healthy, young, pretty, dark-haired, full-faced, but the farm animals – the farm animals – Lordy! She has her own farmstead, a small forest, a brewery, a little mill, a windmill, and cattle and sheep – what else can you say. She'll be getting all of that. So our Ulasovych was in such a hurry that he wouldn't let the horse catch its breath, and he himself, without having eaten his midday meal, covered thirty seven-hundred-sazhen-length versts, racing along, without resting, and as he reached the Bezverkhy Khutir and got off his horse near the cornet's house, he staggered as if he were drunk, and as I mentioned, he didn't stop to eat anywhere.

After greeting Pan Cornet's Son and taking a seat in his house, our fellows got deeply into conversation and proclaimed that their parents were also friendly with each other, so they shouldn't be strangers. Further, the cornet asked our Captain where God was taking him and why? Now our Ulasovych began to lie, because as older people say: as soon as you plan to start wooing, you start lying, too, and not a single man has ever gone wooing without lying. So, our Captain says that apparently, he needs to get some mash for the oxen for the winter (what kind of winter? The Church Feast of Petrivka [Saints Peter and Paul] was just around the corner on June 29), and he heard that in Pan Cornet's Son's brewery, the leftovers from the mash were good and well-tended to, so he came to order some and barter.

"I don't know these matters, so I don't get involved in them. My sister knows better," Pan Cornet's Son told him.

"And where is Olena Yosypivna? If we call her, then we can close the deal with her," Zabryokha said.

"Well! My sister's in the field. They are sowing some millet there, so she's overseeing that because no one knows how to do anything without her. And you, Ulasovych, have some fun. She'll be here by evening. Until she returns, come here, maid! Pour us some plum spirits! We'll drink a glass or two. Since you're already at our place, Pan Captain, spend the night with us, because it's no longer early," Pan Cornet's Son said.

"It's the will of the master!" Mykyta happily replied.

So, they downed a pitcher of plum spirits on their own, and then they tasted a bit of the blackthorn liquor. Our Olena then arrived from the field. She saw that there was a stranger in the house. So, she immediately fluttered about, ordered that carp be brought in from the pond and arranged for dinner to be prepared. She rushed around here and there and gave out the entire work schedule for the next day, and who needed to go for what, and then got dressed so nicely, as was usual for a young lady and daughter of a cornet: she attached a lustrine *zapaska* (sash) to an old *plakhta* (high-waisted woven wrap skirt), put on a silk *yupka* (jacket) with long sleeves and folds at the back, and a ducat coin on a velvet thread around her neck, and red shoes. Then she tied a pretty ribbon on her head and made an entrance, bowing down low to Pan Ulasovych.

Our Zabryokha, when he saw such a lovely young lady, of a kind he had never seen since he was born, such that he never had dreamt of, began to shudder and had no clue what to say, but the cornet reminded him and said:

"So, Pan Captain, here is out mistress of the house. Consult her, she is in charge of everything.

So, what about our Ulasovych? Not a word from his lips. He tried to say something, but he just hemmed and hawed, and began to talk about oxen, then finished talking about doves, thought about grains, and said something about thorns, and when he fell silent, he became really dumbstruck and just swallowed his drool while gazing at such a beauty.

Olena was such a quick-witted damsel. Although Pan Cornet's Son was beating around the bush, she now guessed who he was and why he had come. She said to him, "Okay, laddie. Drink up some blackthorn liqueur for your health and have some dinner, then go to bed, and tomorrow is a new day. As God is willing, we will sleep on it and decide what to do."

Upon hearing this, Zabryokha could not restrain himself from rejoicing, thinking: "That's it, it's all set, tomorrow I just need to bring the embroidered towels with me."[8] He got back to his mug and continued sipping spirits with Pan Cornet's Son who was going to become a monk, but still hadn't rushed to quit drinking. In fact, he loved it even more.

Olena often popped in on the young lads as if it were over this or that business matter, and this time just to scrutinize Mykyta Ulasovych better, to see what was what. When she entered and looked over Pan Captain with her eyes as dark as blackberries. His tongue turned into felt, and he couldn't move it back into his mouth, blushing crimson. After fixing dinner, she didn't come back anymore: the two young lads had dinner by themselves, and, finishing the jug of blackthorn spirits, Pan Cornet's Son wanted to go to bed, until our Zabryokha made champing sounds, coughed, and smacked his lips. He wiped off his mustache and began to say what the deacon composed a long time ago for such an occasion. Here he goes:

"Pan Yosypovych, hark to what I sayeth unto thee: the essence of a single man is incommensurate both in the home and in the household economy. Every breath is esteemed in duality: a man only needeth to marry and have children. And I who art the lowest of men has't taken this thought and insuppressible desire. A flame giveth birth inside me, and I shalt not depart, until I am joined in union with the beautiful, most highly respected Kat…." Here he fell silent. This is what the deacon wrote for him when he thought of courting the

....

[8]   Embroidered towels or cloths are extremely significant in Ukrainian tradition. They are used as part of the engagement ritual as well as the wedding ceremony. The symmetry and symbols of the embroidery are meant to ward off evil and bring happiness to the young couple. For an image of one such "rushnyk" see: https://i.pinimg.com/originals/50/a7/3b/50a73b32e497509cf181bcfdbc4289cc.jpg.

                    HRYHORIY KVITKA-OSNOVYANENKO

priest's daughter from Chernihiv, and Zabryokha recited it to the very end as it was etched by heart in his memory, but then he remembered that the Cornet's daughter was not Kateryna, but Olena, and not highly respected, but – a young damsel, so that's why he fell silent, having messed it up either way. The cornet's son had almost fallen asleep, but he listened closely to this soliloquy and said:

"What are you saying, Pan Captain? Somehow, I don't fathom anything. Was it after drinking the spirits that you became like this?"

Ulasovych sighed and said:

"What a hell of a speech! This is what our deacon wrote for me...."

"But what is it? Yosypovych asked. "Is this a poem, or what?"

"Alas! I myself don't know what it is or what it's for," Zabryokha said.

"So why are you saying such things to me before bedtime? It sends shivers down my spine."

"I wouldn't say anything, but misfortune befell me!"

"What kind of misfortune?" Tell me quickly, I want to go to bed."

"Well! It's for some to sleep and others not to!" Ulasovych said, and, breathing heavily, bowed to the cornet's son deeply and blurted out:

"Give me your sister in marriage!"

"Oy!" said the cornet's son, who began to ponder it, scratching the back of his head and shoulders, then his back, and then said: "I'll see what my sister will say, let's leave this till tomorrow and just sleep on it." Thus, he left him there.

Our Zabryokha went to bed, but he couldn't sleep. Sunrise couldn't come quickly enough. He just needed to hear Olena's answer as soon as possible... Well, somehow, he managed to wait for sunrise, and the two young men arose and met. Then Pan Ulasovych asked:

"What will you say to me, young sir? Does our matter go into effect? If so I would quickly run over to the village elder and then appear here to fulfill my obligation. Tell me, please!"

Our Cornet's Son sniffled and said nothing to him. He just shouted into the adjoining room: "Well, sister! Give us some breakfast, whatever you have there." A servant girl came out of the room, bowed, and set something on the table in front of Pan Ulasovych in a frying pan... baked pumpkin!.. When our Zabryokha saw such an insult, he jumped up from the table and ran out of the house! And here a hired hand was already holding his horse, which was already saddled. He quickly mounted it and began to ride around the house. When he heard people laughing at him, he became even more ashamed. What kind of evil trick was this? Something was dangling from the horse's neck! When he looked, it was a rope with a pumpkin tied to it! He tossed it away, and slapped the horse with his whip, giddyap, giddyap... One thing was the shame: he felt sorry for not getting such a girl, but he didn't even have anything to eat or drink! Now our Ulasovych was already running home with the pumpkin in the same way he ran to the maiden with the thought of taking the embroidered engagement towels. But the misfortune was for himself and his exhausted horse. So, with incredible difficulty, he forced himself home right before midnight and, as I said before, he quickly went to bed.

II

The sad and unhappy Pan Captain Mykyta Ulasovych Zabryokha, was sitting in his attic loft on a bench, and we already know why he was depressed... Eh! We don't know everything though. Won't the one who was clambering into the attic loft of Pan Captain give us more details? And who was it there? What was torturing him so much? First, he stumbled into the door, and then he was pushed back. That long stick that he was carrying in his hands pushed him backwards: when he held it in front of him, right when he peeked in the door, the stick got stuck against the corner. But when he dragged it behind him, he completely entered the attic loft, but it dragged after him and clung to him like a quarrelsome wife behind her drunken old man. But there was no way of carrying it sideways into the attic loft because it was incredibly long. None other than Prokip Ryhorovych[9] Pistryak, the Konotop company's scribe and a sincere friend of Pan Captain of Konotop, Mykyta Ulasovych Zabryokha, clambered in, because without him the Captain would not have a glass of *horilka* (vodka) and would not raise a spoonful of borscht to his mouth. As to giving advice, what Pistryak Ryhorovych says is such and such, it is so and it will always be this way, and he saves you a trip to a hundred fortune tellers. What kind of long stick was he dragging into the attic

....

9   A colloquialized shortened version of the name Hryhorovych (the son of Hryhoriy), the Ukrainian equivalent of the name Gregory. His meaningful last name means "cancer."

loft of Pan Captain? Well now! Let us listen to what they are talking about, then we'll know everything. You'll learn that Pan Pistryak is the scribe: for twelve years he studied with a deacon in school: for a year he studied grammar, for two years he perused liturgical books, for three-and-a-half years he sat over the psalter and learned prayers by heart, and for four-and-a-half years he learned to write and spent a whole year learning the abacus. And in the meantime, he went to the choir loft to learn the tones of chants, Yermolai's dogmatics, Skovoroda's Cherubimic chants, and to harmonize with the deacon, and the readings from the Gospel of Paul. When there is just a tiny bit left to read, he will chant loudly in front of the entire church. and as soon as he gets to really wagging his tongue it isn't small talk but a speech based on the Holy Scriptures. Despite having taken courses in syntax, our Father Kostyatyn listens and listens to him, then shrugs his shoulders and departs from him, saying, "Who knows, my man, what you are saying there!" That's what our scribe, Prokip Ryhorovych Pistryak, was like in Konotop,. And when he begins to talk with Pan Captain Zabryokha, well, you just listen, see whether you can figure out what he's sayin.' I don't know, because he's a man with a learned head; he speaks in a manner that you can't fathom what he's sayin' if you combine ten simple heads together.

So, since Pan Captain sees that Pan Scribe will not be able to get into his attic loft with that long, long stick, he asks:

"Pan Scribe, why the hell are you, skulking into to my attic loft?"

"Aye, my valorous sir, to give a leport [report] about a census-taking of the hundred men consisting of thy troops, who at the present hour standeth under thy leadership, and – may it all crumbleth to dust and ashes! –I can't fit into thy attic loft. We must either breaketh the wall or raiseth the ceiling, because I would not skulk ov'r to thy nobleness!" Pistryak said and began to shuffle around with that long stick again.

"What kind of leport is this thing that's so long? Perhaps, a long stick is in the place of a tail, or what?"

"The long stick, although tis a long stick, tis not merely a long stick, because on't is the repository of souls of the brave Kozak company, which hath resultant from the absence of writing materials and in the presence of the shaking of both mine right and left hand." That's what our Pistryak spit out.

"But tell me simply, Pan Scribe! Oh, I have already grown weary and am feeling ill because I do not fathom anything that you seem to be saying. Here, even without you, nausea has overtaken me, from my liver to my heart, and I sense it coming up," said Pan Captain, and leaned on his hand, and let loose a couple of tears or three.

"Woe is me, Pan Captain!" Pistryak said, "Having thus passed a week causing a ruckus with young maidens in the taverns of our local locality and, missing supper – I hit rock bottom, I was immobile like a clade, and mute like a fish in the sea. And all this sudden news shooketh mine inner womb, and even more so, even more so, when I read and understood the order of the gracious administration to prepare for a campaign to Chernihiv. This they write, Pan Captain, sparing our souls, but not when fear and trembling overcomes us, and we sorrowfully fall onto our bed into death; and for the sake of this, I secretly deliberate, if it will only be to Chernihiv, but who knows? Wilt we go further yet? O woe, woe is me! And I say unto thee: woe is me!"

"O woe, woe Ryhorovych!"

"O woe, woe, Ulasovych!"

Thus, Pan Captain and Pan Scribe lamented that they were sent orders to go to Chernihiv with the entire hundred men of their company and to gather all their equipment and take provisions for themselves and horses for two weeks. Thus Pan Captain laments in his attic loft, and Pan Scribe outside the threshold, and the latter came up with an idea for he was incorrigibly inventive– and said:

"Would thee kindly, Pan Captain, give me the command to break this thrice-cursed long stick, for I am now in the status of the leport, because you yourself are clear-eyed though with unwashed eyes, and you can see theretofore I can't fit into your attic with it."

Pan Ulasovych scratched his head, thought for a long time, and said further:

"That is, in your opinion, the long stick must be made shorter; but you say that this is no longer a long stick, but a leport about our company, so there might be a scolding from the elders; for you yourself know well that Pan Regimental Scribe has been trying to come for us and is planning to attack us with all his might.

"Let us not be fearful, let us not fear the adversary with all his astonishing power. For the sake of this we should oppose him with our sagacity, and this last order given we should fulfilleth without fail, and thus for the order, noble pan, let me breaketh this stick." That was what Pan Pistryak said, twitching his mustache and staring at the ceiling, and then he saw that Pan Mykyta failed to utter a sound from his mouth, because he had not fathomed what was said to him and cried out, "So should I breaketh it?"

"Break it, Pan Scribe!"

There was a crack! Pan Scribe broke the long stick. "I broke it," he said, "and now I can fit in your attic." And while saying this, he clambered into the attic loft and bowed to Pan Captain, and with both hands handed him the broken pieces of the stick and said:

"Please kindly take it!"

"But why are you poking this thing at my eyes, Pan Scribe? Do you want to gouge them out, or what?" Pan Captain asked him, leaning against the wall, and, fearful, thought: "Was Ryhorovych chasing away chimeras in his delirium, like after his drinking binge during Eastertime." "What is it? Tell me simply, without the Holy Writ speaking!"

"Pan Captain, this is in substitution f'r the list of our hundred-man company," said the scribe, "'twas impossible to copy because of the shaking of my hand, yond resulted from the scorn from mine drunkenness with the upper-noted maidens, and because of that I tooketh the long stick and on 't every year marked a Kozak, and this is the correct number: in every group of ten th're art ten Kozaks, and in all such groups of ten th're art also ten, consequently our entire company, it's just as cleareth as that. Pan Captain, deign to make a face-to-face census of your hundred with this long stick. Proclaimeth that your entire company gather near the locality of Kuzmykha, the one-eyed innkeeper, to taketh a look at each and every Kozak.

"Eh, Pan Scribe!" Pan Ulasovych said to him. "I would, as you will, so deign, but I can't count beyond thirty. Do the counting yourself and do as you know how, that's why you're a scribe; and I will sign everything afterward, because I'm a Captain for that, but not to do counting, just to do signing."

Thus, Pan Pistryak began to count; he counted and kept counting, but in the fifth hundred one Kozak was missing. "What strange things?" he screamed. "I have counted those folk, all of those folk were there, and just this one turneth up missing. I'll go mad before I finish this census, whoever of you does not stand up for me before mine eyes but hath run away and hid. None other than, respectfully, Ilko Nalyushnya."

Thus, he went to count the Kozaks, and Pan Captain now rushed to his tankard of pear liqueur and, fretting, drank it down to the last drop without catching his breath. And then Pan Ryhorovych with his stub of a stick clambered into the door, all cheerful, to comfort Pan Captain, and said instead: "Do not worry, my good man! Of all our Kozaks are together, not one scampered off anywhere; here is where they are." He started to count – again in the fifth group of ten there was an absent Kozak! How Ryhorovych began to stomp his feet, how he tugged his forelock, how he began to cuss the father, mother, and entire family of that whoreson Kozak, who was hiding while he was bringing his leport to the house to Pan Captain. When he counted outside, everyone was accounted for, but when he counted in the house, then one, always in the fifth group of ten, disappeared, like he never existed! Pan Pistryak returned to the company, counted the Kozaks – all were there; he returned to Pan Captain, counting according to the long stick that he had notched for each of them – one was missing; someone had taken off. Again, he'd return to the hundred-man troop to smack the one who was hiding, because everyone was there then, but one was always missing in the attic loft. About ten times he saw this happen. The poor wretch was already puffing and panting from running from the house then to the hundred-man troop, to the point that Pan Ulasovych had already put his coat on and took his hat to go to the company, since Pan Scribe had one Kozak taking off each and every time, and who that was – was not known, of course, because everyone was at the assembly and holding each other by the belt, so that no one could run away while they were being counted by the long stick.

"That's enough fooling around, Ryhorovych. Let's go together. If everyone is there, and one is missing on the long stick, damn it! Let him be missing, as long as everyone remains alive," the Captain said, and stared intently at the scribe, to see what he had to say on the matter and how he would erupt at him over such a trifle, as often happened.

Prokip Ryhorovych listened to this for a long time, pointed his finger, and then he smacked his lips, jumped up, and shouted: "Well, here is how it is! With my entire being I regret that such a reverie comes out of my head and bow down to the impassable thickness of the wilderness. But Pan Captain, you will have to become a regimental judge for such an unbridled and wise decision, that I wouldst not have taken. Let us go, sire! Now my innermost being has risen knowing that the entire hundred-man troop is there, and, upon having completed the matter, no time is better to have a good meal."

Thus, they set off. Aha! And our Pan Captain became a little more cheerful that somehow without thinking or guessing he managed to come up with something, all the more so that Prokip Ryhorvych Pistryak himself, the Konotop company's scribe, praised him for something he had come up with for the very first time since birth. And Ryhorovych followed after the Captain, and pondered and thought to himself: "This is already going in the direction of misfortune when Pan Captain is cleverer than I. Why would he needeth a scribe when he himself cogitates things and signs them, too? 'Tis just not clear if he himself will write and, perhaps, do accounts. I won't give in!.. I'll turn his day around." They went to Kuzmikha's tavern, and the hundred-man company was standing there and, taking off their hats, bowed to Pan Captain.

"Greetings, kids! Are you all here?" Pan Captain asked them, and folding his arms, he looked them over right in their faces, as if he were counting or examining everyone; though I'm saying, he couldn't count beyond thirty, and did not know a single Kozak by countenance and did not understand which of them was Demko or Protsko.

"Greetings, father! The gathered group shouted to him. "We are all here, every single one of us."

"Count them, scribe, to see if anyone is hiding," the Captain commanded, puffing up like an owl.

And here again was misfortune for the scribe Ryhorovych. When he put the long stick together, according to the notches on it, all the Kozaks were present.

"Which of you devils was gadding about when I visited Pan Captain?" Pistryak shouted from his heart and even stomped his foot.

"Come on, Ryhorovych," Pan Ulasovych told him as he smiled. "All the Kozaks are here, not a single one has escaped from the long stick. When you broke the long stick, it cracked right on a Kozak. And holding the two halves, you were not able to count one of them because of that."

And the group of Kozaks, while listening to this, guffawed: "Yes, noble father, yes!" they shouted and said: "That's what our scribe is like, I see! Oh, to hell with him."

"To hell with thee, with the Kozaks, and with the long stick, and the counting, and the commanders," Ryhorovych shouted to the entire street, as if he himself would explode from rage. He seized that long stick, broke it, smashed it into pieces, and threw it into the Kozaks' faces, saying: "Damn you, to hell with you, sons of whores! May you have hundreds or more fevers and e'en more boils and sores if you can find anybody smarter than me among ye. Wherefore doth ye needeth me?" And he again began to quote from the Holy Writ: "I shalt goeth out into the wilderness and settle in the mountains of Ararat, at the remains of the sea.[10] Damn you!"

Here Pan Captain stopped him, took him by the arm, and said,

"Enough of being angry, Ryhorovych. Just once I mocked you, and you are already taking offense. Remember when you gave me the leport, and not knowing how to write or read anything, I signed it rashly. And Pan Colonel wrote, saying, "Konotop Captain, Pan Mykyta, you are a fool! But I didn't get angry with you for that, even though you kept reminding me of that and laughed in my face. Enough already, enough! Let's go have our lunch...."

"Go ahead and gorge on thy meal, saveth thy holy bread. May the one who pulleth my leg be choked!..," our Pistryak clenched his hands, completely angry, and dragged himself home without looking back, muttering to himself: "Thou

---

[10] Ryhorovych seems to be basing his quotation in part on Isaiah 43:17-19, which in the KJV reads: "I will make a way in the wilderness and rivers in the desert."

shalt be choked at which hour I shalt begin my nefarious deeds…Thou shalt be conveyed into trouble… There will be a Captain in Konotop, just not Zabryokha… They will boweth down to Pistryak."

"What shall we do?" The Kozaks began to grumble upon seeing that all their superiors had either gone mad or the devil knows what: the scribe, as if he had eaten the devil's weed, dragged himself off to his home, and Pan Captain bowed his head and started off to his own house. So, they turned to Pan Captain to ask what they should do and why they had gathered.

"The devil knows!" Mykyta Ulasovych shouted at them, cursing out both their fathers and mothers. "Damn you, stop bothering me. Go the hell wherever you want, even to the gallows. What kind of order can I give when the scribe has gone mad? He has a leport" (Pan Ulasovych called any paper a leport, not knowing how to say it, whether there was an order, or anything else). "Let him have a good sleep, for he often speaks nonsense,"," he said "then we'll figure it out, but not now." And he set off homeward quietly.

Looking at this, the Kozaks began to leave: some to the taverns, some to the haystacks, to rest after such a disciplining; and others rushed off to the gardens to stir up the girls….

III

Upon returning after the inspection of the Kozak company, the sad and unhappy Konotop Pan Captain, Mykyta Ulasovych Zabryokha, was sitting on a bench, but no longer in the attic loft but in the living room. Add to the calamity that the cornet's daughter Olena Yosypovna had brought to him the day before a baked pumpkin, as offensive as strong snuff placed under his nose and he had not had anything to eat or drink since that day; he needed to gather his company for a campaign, all the way to Chernihiv. But I say, after such a misfortune, a new calamity befell him, for he had angered his company's scribe Prokip Ryhorovych Pistryak, and having become angry, the latter would no longer give him any advice when the leaders send a leport about anything or how things are there; so what could he do? With such a misfortune, how could he not be sullen and cheerless? Ehe! He's there sitting in the living room on a bench, at the end of the table, his head drooping nearly to his knees! He sat there for more than an hour if not two... And then the servant girl called him from another room:

"My good sir, why are you, sad and sitting there in silence? Isn't it time to have dinner?"

"I don't feel like!" Ulasovych responded and breathed a heavy sigh that sounded throughout the house, propping his head up with his hand.

In a short while, the servant girl came out of the room, and sweetly looked at him, saying joyfully:

"Or maybe you've already had your midday meal, yes, maybe, or you want to have your lice picked... or something?"

"I don't feel like it!" Ulasovych gave the same answer without looking at her.

Frowning, the servant girl returned to the room and sat down in the corner, grumbling: "Perhaps he must have visited the priest's place already and must have eaten there; 'cause those priests' daughters take a shine to men no matter who," and sitting there by herself, she rebuked the priests' daughters.

And to be sure, Mykyta Ulasovych sat and thought his own thoughts. And suddenly... A grating noise!.. Someone had entered the house... Pan Captain glanced! None other than our Ryhorovych entered. Apparently, he had gotten over his anger? No, he hadn't gotten over his anger, but came with a plot to Pan Mykyta. Listen here to what happened further... So, when he entered, he stood silently by the door.

Pan Ulasovych wasn't overjoyed either. As he eyed his great friend, he thought: "He now is no longer angry and will give me advice in my time of misfortune." But Ryhorovych didn't go there: he kept standing by the door silently without a word.

"What do you have to say, Ryhorovych?" Pan Captain asked the scribe. But he gave him an answer, without moving from the spot where he was standing:

"What do you command, Pan Captain?"

"Oh, well, go to hell with this pan captaining. Don't you know my nature? Before the Kozaks, yes, I am a Captain, and you are a scribe. But when we are together in the house, we are brothers. Sit down, we'll have our midday meal," Ulasovych said.

"Thank you! I've already eaten." And Ryhorovych nodded his head, saying the following.

"Oh, what a liar!," the Captain says. "So sit yourself down, I'll eat, and you'll drink some pear liqueur. It's good, last year's, we've just started drinking it this week, it's so good that once you have a sip – you'll want to drink more."

"I have quaffed the threefold cup of calamity," said the scribe, sighing, "and I have no room for more of the miserable pear liqueur, wherefore it will swirl in my mouth like wormwood."

"Pan Scribe, why are you, " the Captain began to say kindly to him, "in tarnation still breathing poison on me? For what reason and what is this about? Not even an old gypsy would be able to figure it out."

"It is nonsensical, Pan Captain, to conjoin all the Pharaoh's host with us, the faithful. Even without a gypsy here you can figure things out. Especially when you bring upon me a thrice-damned humiliation, for what is there after this? Like a steed and half-breed! Fie! Trolly lolly!"

"What kind of a humiliation do you mean, Pan Scribe! Just that you couldn't figure out that damned long counting stick...."

"May it perish with a crackling sound in a burning stove! And ye, Pan Captain, looking at the mockery of me, should have kept silence and instead of humiliating me in public, roaring like a lion, ye should have told me the truth in private, so that our Kozaks had not ridiculed me crying out: "Our scribe is a fool, he couldn't figure out that our long stick is easy to break." After all, I toldeth ye well in the attic loft: I wast inebriated and had not yet sobered another time; and yet if my hands shaketh, like the leaves of trees, then what would my head be with all its thoughts? It was as a thrice-agitated sea. Pan Captain, ye should have hidden the transgressions of your brother; ye should have told him with your lips to his ear, and not for all of Kozakdom to hear."

"So, you are right, Ryhorovych; now I myself see that it is so," said our Ulasovych. And it had always been this way: whatever Pistryak would come up with, whatever he would suggest, Pan Captain would be quick to agree: "Yes, it is so." That is how he now agreed with him, and, looking at him right in the eye, saw that Ryhorovych ate all this up like dumplings with butter; so, he began to speak to him more boldly and to joke, and said: "Sit down, my friend; Why the hell are you loitering around the threshold like a puppy tied on a leash? Come, come; sit near me; I'll eat, and you drink down some of the pear liqueur. Pazka! Brink in a full pitcher of the pear liqueur! – Pazka left her quarters and, crossing through the living room, already looked cheerfully at the young gentleman of the house. And Prokip Ryhorovych thought for a bit, then he began to walk around the house singing a psalm under his breath: "Thou holdest mine eyes waking[11]." And then, he took a deep breath and went up to Pan Ulasovych, and while twitching his mustache, he began to say to him:

"Yes, indeed, I am not lying. And let our mother earth swallow me while I sleepeth, if I doth lie e'en a whit. A sole commander is not allowed to cause suffering to his scribe with his right hand; because every man shall have a head, a head hath a mind, a mind hath free will, and this will commands the right hand, the left hand, and every bodily member. But this example has the following understanding: the man is – the Konotop company; the head is – Pan Captain; the mind in his head art – I, a miserable scribe; I haveth free will, in essence, a gift, to write, that would the regimental scribe himself write something similar. Morevoer, if a man doth not obey his head, there is additionally, the mind in the head; in that time he is plagued by confusion and trembling; and this is how it should be. But if the company does not have to obey Pan Captain, but to the contrary are supposed to make it worse for me and, more than anything, not to shield my lack of knowledge, but also to mock me? Oh! For what reason am I in the world?"

---

[11] Psalm 72:4 in the KJV.

And having spit this out, he sat down on a bench, propping up himself with his hand, looking very sad. Mykyta Ulasovych felt sorry for him and said:

"If the truth be told, brother, I have not fathomed a dang thing that you have said to me; for you see, this is from the Holy Writ and you know that I don't get it, and that it hinders me right now when someone addresses me with it. Do me a kindness, do not be angry with me, and speak to me from your heart but not from the Holy Writ, and just say it simply. Let's not make it more complicated. I don't have to tell you that we have calamity after calamity, and here also have to go on a campaign. Let us discuss what we should do about that leport...."

"Who the devil knows what ye are saying," the scribe buzzed at Pan Captain, "Is it appropriate for the leadership to write a leport to subordinates? Leaders give orders. Innumerable times I sayeth thus unto ye, and all in vain."

"Still, it is a leport, nothing more. I am glad that I have been able to pronounce the word 'leport,' but the other thing you are saying, I will not be able to utter. So, the devil with the leports, but let's discuss how to go on the campaign. After all, the entire hundred-man company is here, good; well then, tell me what to do?"

"Hmm, Hmm!" Ryhorovych began to cough as he remembered how he had tried to count the company of the hundred men. So, he began scheming to frame and ruin the captain, and to better himself.... Well, let's not speak beforehand, but listen to how it goes. Thus he said, "Whatsoever Pan Captain commands, I must fulfilleth without fail."

"But do me a favor, Ryhorovych, I've had enough of this!" said Pan Captain and sat down at the table, because Pazka had brought in a full pitcher of the pear liqueur. "Sit down with me," he says, and if you don't want to sup with me, drink down some of the pear liqueur and don't bother me about business."

Hence the Captain silently dined, and the scribe sat and continued to sit, remaining silent; then he grabbed a spoon, and he began, as he says, first to devour hot borscht with all manner of small fish, and millet kasha in oil, then chilled borscht with tench fish, and then soup with burbot and wheat dumplings, and baked crucian carp, all in the same bowl... and nothing more. Although our Ryhorovych had eaten at home no less than what he now consumed at Pan Captain's, it was nothing for him. He received a good schooling from the deacon, who would take him to lunches so that his voice got higher and stronger with every meal, ringing like a bell that you could hear throughout the entire street as it chimed in your ears; then our Ryhorovych became accustomed to multiple lunches, and he was not afraid to have at least six lunches. It was the same with Ulasovych. When he saw a good dish especially with fresh fish, he began to gobble it down, as if he had not eaten anything that morning.

When he ate, he ate heartily till his ears burst, then he grabbed the pitcher and, without pouring it into a tankard, drained all the pear liqueur out of it. Further, having risen up from the table, he gave thanks to God and to the master of the house, sat down on a bench, cleared his throat, smoothed his mustache, and said:

"Thanks be to the fine repast and outstanding liqueur, I consign my sorrow to heavenly oblivion. Let us not mention that thrice-damned long stick, the breaking of which made one missing Kozak. May it be damned! Yes, it will be a thricely damned anathema, and it will burn in a Chaldean oven, and even better, in a fiery Gehenna. Let us say what we do and do what we say. Let it be known to thee, kind Pan, that tis impossible for us to go on a campaign! Oh!" and he was about to explain why so....

"Wow!" Pan Ulasovych shouted with joy and ran up to him to question him some more, saying: "How is this possible? And the leport?...."

"Fie! Thou always beateth upon the same drum!" Ryhorovych says. "'Tis like speaking to a solid brick wall, you keepeth on and on about the leport. Well, 'tis all for nothing! No matter how they try to convince us, we cannot go: it is not convenient for us, we have not the time!"

"Why don't we have time? Do me a kindness, explain what you mean: why don't we have time?"

"Hmm, hmm!" Ryhorovych replied as he coughed and thought, "whatev'r do we have to do with Chernihiv and the regimental leaders, if the entire world is doomed?"

"How is that?" Pan Mykyta asked, frightened. "Why is the world doomed? What is this? I am the Konotop Captain, and I do not know that the world is doomed? So, please tell me why it is doomed, and can we somehow defend or buttress it?"

"Doomed!" Pistryak said with a sigh. "No one can give counsel regarding succor to all who see and wonder,. Pan Captain Ulasovych, look and be horrified! It hasn't rained for three se'en nights and a half, the heavens will shut over the earth deprived of rain; all will be transformed into dust and ashes, all vegetation will dry up, and just dust will swirl in our universe and – Oh, woe is me, a sinner! – This dust takes up residence in my until now unsullied nose and makes me sneeze, akin to the intolerable and thrice-damned– fie!— strong snuff. I have been pure and not besmirched by it since I left from my mother's womb, and it would be so until this day. O, woe is me!"

"So why should the world be doomed," said Pan Zabryokha, "because you are sneezing, Pan Scribe?"

"Howev'r, sneezing!" Ryhorovych said, shaking his head. "Not only am I sneezing, but even the regimental scribe himself, and moreover, our most radiant and most noble Pan Hetman will sneeze, when this vilely evil snuff and this accursed cotton dust that is swept up by the air.settles in the nose of his Radiance. And if we do not create a sudden downpour, everything will dry up and perish! The greenery and grasses will also wither, and no grains will grow; thus, we will not just suffer, but instead face a sudden death from hunger and thirst. I rationally say unto you: we must bring rain to our impoverished land!"

"Thus far, I figured out only half of what you are saying to me, Pan Scribe. After all, are you saying that we have no rain? Thus, what can we to do? Can we know the powers of heaven and make it rain?"

"We can!" Our Pistryak shouted at the top of his lungs, and then pounded his fist on the table and shouted even harder: "And I say unto ye, we can."

"And pray tell me, pray tell how, Pan Scribe,?" Pan Zabryokha asked. "I am also the Konotop Captain, and there are things I do not know up to this day."

"Pay attention, Pan Captain! And be so kind, Mykyta Ulasovych, to fathom what I will say unto ye, so that I do not repeat myself ten times. There are impious hussies in the world, evidently from the tribe of Canaan, Canalian in translation, who submit to Beelzebub and his demonic wiles, and they become engaged in witchcraft, during the nighttime, when we are lying down and asleep. These wicked beings leave their houses and donning a white shirt, letting their hair down, and coming to their neighbors' and other inhabitants' abodes enter the milkhouse, better to simply say, the barn, and thither they approach the cows, and milk them, along with timid sheep, and fleet-footed mares, and wicked female dogs, and, moreover, they milk scratchy cats, malicious mice, depraved frogs... and all things that breathe, creep, and jump that have milk-producing accoutrements, milking them only with infamous, ungodly artistry. And having gathered all these types of milk, with diabolical bewitchment, they transform it into spells so as to create everything according to their own purpose, such as: stealing young suckling infants from the womb and instead putting thither a frog, or a mouse, or even a puppy; sowing enmity and discord in a spousal household; arousing lust in a young man for a maiden and in her for him, and other manner of unsurmountable evil; and foulest of all, closing up downpours inside the heavens and interdicting the rain from irrigating the land, so that humanity would perish. Do you understand now, good sir, how this tribulation has reached our holy land, if we have not had even a drop of rain to this very day? Come now, do not yawn and say, hast thou understood my words?"

"Why not?" Although I am … yawning… I have already understood. Did you tell me that we have not had rain or what?

"Yes, yes. But because of whom does this happen?"

"Is it because of… the frogs, or… because of someone… I did not quite get it."

"What do you mean frogs? Through the witches I say unto you."

"To hell with them, do not mention them to me, Pan Scribe! Although the evening is distant, I will be terrified the entire night and will not sleep if you frighten me. I will be utterly afraid of the witches."

"It does not befit us to be fearful of them, but we must eliminate them to the third generation."

"How do you eliminate them, Ryhorovych? You go after her, and she will turn into a ball and throw herself at your legs, knock you down, and then disappear. Hasn't this happened? More than a few elderly people say something about this, so, after listening to them, your shivers will keep you up all night."

"Not only do the old people have stories, I can also relate to you a story of this kind of mockery. Once, I was at evening festivities about which the young people informed me, having eaten our fill of animal flesh, traipsed around quite a bit, and having drunk without measure, to as much a degree as possible. I was still in a sober condition, walking to my place of abode, but before reaching the hut of old Tsymbalykha, something started to swirl at my feet; my head began to spin, and I staggered and flailed hither and thither, and was unable to keep my balance. I fell down and lay there on the spot and fell asleep motionless, as if I were dead, until I awakened in the morning. This was nought other than an attack by an accursed witch. It would be pleasant to bind them well, so they will return the rain from their secret hiding places and water the earth.

"How can we, Pan Ryhorovych, go after them so that they return the rains and not play any dirty tricks on us?"

"Let us not be fearful or afraid!" Pan Pistryak said. "Blessed and eternal glory worthy of remembrance, your venerably remembered parent and father, Ulas Panasovych, the magnificent Pan Captain of the most courageous Konotop company, by whose sagacious leadership the entire universe was amazed – and let him rest in peace – he ruled wisely and honorably with those ancient wenches of Egypt, better to say, witches. You should act, good man, without fail according to his example.

"And what did my late Pan Father do to them? Just say it, so that perhaps I can do the same, too?"

"Your much-commemorated, admirable father used to drown them in the river. And if some witch would not go to the bottom, a millstone was hung on her neck because this type of evil creature does not sink. Will you order us, Pan Captain, to drown them?"

"Yes, drown them! Why spare anything?" Ulasovych decided.

"Thy good will be fulfilled," said the scribe, "this morning I will command everything be done according to the traditional way in such cases, and everything will be splendid; thus, we will no longer be going on a campaign to Chernihiv?"

"No, Pan Scribe, we will not go. Only... How do we dispense with them?"

"We'll dispense with them, Pan Captain; and for the sake of this we will dispatch a messenger on foot, the lame Ilko Khverlushchenko, who will limp over to the high command with a leport that will say that we cannot undertake a campaign, because we are cautiously plunging witches into the abyss of our pond, in order to save the entire world from destruction, because they are hiding the rain in their cupboards.

"Good, good, Pan Scribe, we've very wisely come up with idea. Go and write the leport, and I, after talking to you, have gotten the urge to go into a deep sleep. I should have told you about my misfortune, but I am not able to ...can't help falling asleep," said Pan Captain, yawning widely.

Here Prokip Ryhorovych set off to give the order on how to drown the witches tomorrow, and Mykyta Ulasovych lay down to rest without even lice-picking to help him fall asleep.

That played right into Pan Pistryak's hands. He did with Pan Captain what he needed to do and what he had long wanted to do. He made a fool of him, so that he would not listen to the orders of the high command and not go on the campaign to Chernihiv, maybe not fight back against the Tatars or the Liakhs [Poles]; and while the lame Khverlushchenko with one leg would limp to the high command who would read that Pan Konotop Captain, instead of taking action, started to drown witches, they would think that although he had always been foolish and he was now completely crazy... "They will surely replace him, and will designate no one other than me as the new captain." Thus, Ryhorovych thought. And clearing his throat like when Pan Deacon was about to read a midnight prayer, he thought to himself: "To the hostile wenches and young wives, who have done insult to me, or those who do not obey... methinks I know those kind... I will get recompense... I know such people... I will give them a good dousing! Glory be that my fool cringes and crawls into his misfortune as though into a yoke. Now, Prokip, just gallop onward!" He sighed and said loudly to himself: "This is good recompensel for our brother, a cunning and intelligent scribe, a, when such a fool is in charge like our always-remembered Pan Zabryokha! Neither the right nor the left hand will become impoverished, and both the pocket and belly will be filled. Give us no less, O Lord, such as he!"

IV

It was a sad and unhappy morning in the famous Kozak regimental town of Konotop. Though before sunrise, before the
moon had hidden itself well enough, a buzzing, scurrying
about, shouting, and hubbub arose all over the streets and
then it died down, and all the people disappeared, so there
was no one in the houses or in the streets, like a tavern on
Easter before morning services. You could hear only the cows
lowing with as much spirit as they had, but the milkmaids did
not go to milk them and did not even think of driving them
to the herd. Hearing their mothers lowing, the calves in the
barns mooed and vocalized, as if asking to be released from
their pens more quickly. The sheep were bleating and so were
the goats, stomping and running around the fencing, looking
for a spot where they could jump out and lead the sheep to
follow behind them. Horses neighed so that the entire village
could hear them; the echo even went up to the stars. The
geese honked, the ducks quacked, the hens clucked – because
all living creatures suffered without human aid. And hearing
such a ruckus, the dogs at first barked, then began to howl.
Little children who couldn't yet walk crawled around their
closed house and, grabbing onto an embankment next to the
hut with their tiny little hands, straining, would get up on
their tiny little legs and find a splinter, and, taking it in his
mouth, sucked it instead of a bone, but when he began to turn
it in his hands, he could not hold on and... plopped again onto
the clay floor, and cried. Then, you know, a puppy, approaching closely and being hungry, came up and licked his tears

and the tip of his nose, and licked inside his mouth, then the child, not knowing how to defend himself from the puppy, cried more intensely, thinking that someone would come to defend him and clean him... All in vain! The huts all over the small town are locked; carts, plows, harrows, wooden plows, where they were lined up in the evening, stand there; the oxen, having eaten their straw, saw that no one would water or harness them, slipped away and walked off along the streets, and where they saw meal cakes or chamomile and all sorts of weeds, that's where they grazed....

Not a single student was there near the deacon's school! Waiting for them, Pan Symeon walked next to the school, arranging funerals and remembering the *kutya*[12] with honey, and carefully stared at the yard of old Kyryk, who the day before had already had last rites conducted over him and had been anointed with holy oil. Was it not smoke coming from the chimney, perhaps, they already were making a funeral repast if he had already died. Wishful thinking! The chimney pipe was not smoking and no one was running about in the yard.

"Ehe, ehe! will he rise up from his sickbed?" Pan Symeon thought and reasoned, walking about in the yard, how healthy and long-lived people have become so that he would remember how nice it was to live then during the times of cholera, and then he would sigh heavily, enter the hut, and begin to get whips ready for the schoolchildren in order to unburden his soul on someone....

There were huge weeds in the garden patches, and no one thinks of weeding, though hoes were lying nearby; and between the beds with seedlings and beetroots and other kinds of vegetables, there are sows with their piglets having a real

....

12 A sweet wheatberry dish served during Ukrainian holidays, particularly at Christmas and Easter. It is also used for funeral repasts.

feast and not bothering to leave anything for the master and mistress of the house. They eat to their hearts' content and with their noses dig new beds that the lady of the household would be hard-pressed to put in order in two days; and now there is no one to chase them out, because there just is no one... Moreover the village pubs themselves are empty. The innkeeper dozes on a bench because there is absolutely nobody to drink *horilka*, and there is no wife and daughters-in-law so no one forbids him from dozing. The glasses, which he had rinsed out and arranged last evening, were standing there, and no one would turn their foot toward the village pub....

But why is it so in the famous Kozak regimental town, Konotop, why has it become so quiet and sad that no one can hear a single voice? And you will not meet a single man on a single street, as if – may God have mercy! – have all the people in the entire town died, or – and it's no better than death – perhaps the Crimean Tatars captured them? Where did they disappear to that that they abandoned both their home and belongings and their little children? Well, that might account for the women: they have no problem getting together in a group and spending the entire day nattering away and not worrying much about their menfolk and children being left without supper but there is not a single man in the village. Moreover: you won't come across a child who is already able to walk. Where are they? Aye! Here they are, all of them gathered around the pond staring at it... And what are they staring at, hey, hey! Not even the eldest in our village can understand what's happening in Konotop... What's going on there?

In the middle of the pond four heavy posts were driven, they were tied with ropes at the top and again somehow neatly and nicely intertwined; and in each post, a hole was drilled at the top with a rope threaded through it... And people rode around the pond in boats, but they were not fishermen because they didn't have nets fish traps on their boats, but ropes too... And what was on the bank, so that all the people from the famous Kozak regimental town of Konotop gathered there as the sun had not yet risen and the bad moon had not set... That's where you could find those mothers who had abandoned their homes, their little children, their piglets, poultry and cows, and had not heated their ovens. That is where you could find those men who had left their infirm wives at home, and had forgotten that they needed to drive their livestock to the field... Absolutely everyone had gathered to see what would happen here....

But there were so many of them here! All over the shore and all around the hills, they were packed in there like grain collected in sacks. And the lads and young bachelors, who could not see anything from behind the crowd of people, climbed onto willow trees and covered them like jackdaws...

And Lordy! The cry, and murmur from the people! It's as though the water was churning when a downpour breaks a dam: everyone speaks simultaneously, and no one listens to anyone else. Sure enough these are our buzzing women! This was where you could see the innkeeper's wife and her daughters-in-law, without whom the innkeeper can sleep; they chat, chirp, tell tales: who was in their pub yesterday, how much they drank for cash, how much on credit, who pawned what, who had a fight with whom, whose wife came and took him from the tavern, who chased after his wife and knocked off her headdress[13] from the back of her neck and whose hair was publicly exposed; how deceitful girls bought *horilka* for themselves instead of supposedly for their fathers, and drank it with young men secretively in the orchards and, getting drunk, rolled and wrestled and... "That's enough!

....

[13] Traditional headdress required of married women at the time in Ukraine. For examples of the different types see: https://uk.wikipedia.org/wiki/%D0%9E%D1%87%D1%96%D0%BF%D0%BE%D0%BA.

Don't tell everything!" the innkeeper's wife shouted at her daughter-in-law and fell silent. But maybe she wanted to say something good....

And there, on the other side of the pond next to the willow trees, instead of going to school where some should rather have been reading from the Book of Hours[14] or memorizing poems from the psalter or composing verses for chants,[15] schoolchildren gathered in a group and composed a ditty about their deacon, secretively singing it to the sixth liturgical tone:

> Come all ye worshippers from all around,
> And look around, all the deacons are drunk in town,
> Most of all, Symeon got drunk and fell down,
> From the *horilka* he doesn't see a thing,
> And in the choir loft he's unable to sing,
> Today he forgot to read the psalter,
> He only can thrash us near the altar,
> This day his wife washed his head,
> And made the light in his brain turn dead...

And upon hearing these words Pan Symeon lashed out at them with the whip that he brought from home; then he chased them to school with it, and while chasing them, swore that for this prank, besides Saturday thrashings which the law approves, he would thrash them himself for a whole month on Sundays, the Lord's Day.

....

[14]   A daily prayer book and book of religious readings somewhat analogous to the *Book of Common Prayer* in the English tradition.

[15]   "Irmos" is a Greek term found in the Divine Liturgy and means "link." These verses provide the rhythm and melody for Scriptural canticles. Information on them can be found here https://mci.archpitt.org/liturgy/Canons.html.

And what's going on there near the mill! Hey, hey! There were many as thirty Kozaks, some with a lance, some with a whip, some with a good cudgel, some with a fighting stick, and all of them holding firmly onto the ropes, with seven wenches tied to those ropes... I'll tell you who these wenches were.

The first was age-old Priska Chyryachka, who when she was young sat chained to the wall next to the church many times [for the immoral acts that she committed], sent off three men to the netherworld, and transformed all the farm animals into potions and roots for all sorts of medicines, and healed people either from fevers, or from rheumatism or parotitis, because since she was young she has been strangling mole-rats – to cure a cold, to remove fear, to lick an evil eye away, or to treat upset stomachs... Is there anything she did not know? And all kinds of infirm people came to her from every corner as far as twenty versts away. She would help one destined to live to recover whereas the doomed would die right after sipping her potion. Then Priska said, "He was not so sick for him to be alive!" Once Pan Pistryak asked her to give him a love potion, so that any maiden or eligible young woman upon whom he cast an eye would fall in love with him; so he drank up those potions and went to the evening parties but just as the party was in full swing he got so sick that he didn't even make his way home. From that time on, he became her persecutor!

Khymka Ryabokobylykha was another one, an old person who was mesmerized. If something that belongs to you is missing, do not think of going to a fortune teller. She will outwit even the most skillful of their kind and pin the theft on whomever she is angry with and wants to blame. And how can you not believe her when she saw in a trance what suffering there was in the netherworld for thieves, and snuff takers, and liars, and loose women. Thus, if someone was brought to the town hall, who was caught in the melon field with cucumbers or in the pantry with pig lard, and then Khymka said that it was not he who did the stealing, right away they would release him and they would go after whoever Khymka said, even though that person was not in the village either. That's how she tattled on Pan Pistryak – what's more, not even the high-ranking kind was spared! – that he allegedly stole some bees from a man. He got away with it, of course, as a scribe, and since then he has had her in his sights.

The third was the so very old and ancient Yavdokha Zubykha! However, the old geezers who are barely able to drag their feet, relate that when they were young fellas, she was as old then as she is now. So as not to lie, she was about fifty years old. People say that during the daytime she is old, and as the sun sets, she grows younger; and at the darkest midnight she becomes a really young girl, and then begins to grow older and becomes as old by sunrise as she was yesterday. Anyhow, when she gets younger, she puts on a white blouse and lets her hair down, like a maiden, and goes to milk cows, sheep, goats, mares, dogs, and cats in the village, and in the swamps – frogs, lizards, vipers... Indeed, she will milk anything and everything you can imagine! Although there is nothing there, she will take what she wants. Once Pan Scribe Ryhorovych was reading aloud some missive from his superiors to the community, and although he had been drinking to excess for five days before that he read it well and, just as his voice was getting stronger, Zubykha came by, looked at him, and just smiled. What happened? He tossed the paper on the ground, pulled up the hems of his garments, and started to dance and jump in front of the people. There was laughter galore! And since then, Pan Pistryak becomes that way; even when he just drinks a little, he starts acting very weirdly. That's what Yavdokha was like.

The fourth was Pazka Psiuchykha, who was not that old. Unlike the others, she always conjured secretly, without drawing attention to herself. She could be seen when everyone had gone to sleep. She would come outside and wave her hand. The clouds would go where she waved her hand. And she would not take anything from whoever would come to her for magic, or any herbal medicine or anything like that, even if they brought her some treat, and would say: "I know nothing; go away!" Well, well! So, she doesn't know!

The fifth was Domakha Karlyuchkivna. In her young years she was so pretty, there were no words to describe her. She was small in stature, although no matter what house she entered, she would reach the ceiling with her head. She was thin and long-legged; the hair on her head was as frizzy as uncombed wool, and when her mouth was agape, an entire shovel could fit in. She had a tiny nose, like a hazel grouse. And as she looked out from Konotop with her immense eyes, one was directed at Kyiv and the other at Bilahorod, and they were covered as if with the milky film of sour cream; and her face as white as an oxcart driver's shirt. Additionally, her face was scratched all over as if had been raked. With such raving beauty she remained unmarried. First she craved priest's sons, then after that she lowered her sights onto scribes from the town hall, she then took to desiring a tillerman after that, all in vain! Even a sheepherder would not set his eyes on her. There was nothing she could do! She tied up her gray hair, went over to live in a deserted house on a meadow above a swamp, and began to conjure and play nasty tricks on people. Don't you dare upset her! If you do not bow down to her in the usual way, or shove her without looking, or something else, right away she will screech out: "You will see, you son of a dog; just wait!" It happens thus: either while you're walking, you will stumble, or you will choke while you're having dinner, or you will lose something while drunk, and you will not get away with it! So, as they say if not there then here, if not now, then in a year, but you won't be spared. It's terrifying to say more about her. Damn her! God forbid if you see her in your dreams....

The sixth was Vekla, the daughter-in-law of old Shtyrya, and the seventh was Ustya Zholobykha. Let someone else tell you about them, I don't have the time. For some reason the people of Konotop have begun to stir and swarm, and some separated and opened up a path to the pond, for when a sow is being roasted she forgets about her little piggies.

V

Sad and unhappy, puffed up like a rooster in front of his hens, Pan Captain Mykyta Ulasovych Zabryokha of the bold Konotop Company went to the Konotop pond. Although he wore a blue Circassian caftan with wide sleeves folded back and a Tatar belt dividing it in half, with a small knife attached to a chain, his face washed, and his beard shaved, and a hat on his head, his eyes were sleepy and puffy. It was apparent that he was drinking hard all night. And it was so: the whole dang night he was slamming down a big pitcher because of his sadness, and his maidservant Pazka, you know, kept topping off his goblet. So, after that kind of night, when you do not get enough sleep, then your head buzzes like a beehive for a long time. I know this well. So why should he not be sad and unhappy? Although he went up to people, all of whom took off their hats in front of him and paid deference to him, he walked alone, pouting, and he looked at no one. Only he puffed out his cheeks, so that everyone knew that he was the elder leader here.

So, he went up to the pond, cast his eyes here and there, and shouted menacingly:

"What?"

"The finale is afoot," the scribe, Prokip Ryhoryovych Pistryak, called out to the Konotop Kozak captain standing near the sentries who were guarding the cluster of witches and watching closely so that none of them, turning either into a magpie or a pig, would take to her heels. When he heard the voice of his superior, he immediately took off his hat, walked up to him, and bowed down low, saying: "How sayest thee, Pan Captain, in thy commanding action, in thy diurnal abode!"

"Thank you!" Ulasovych loudly responded, without sorting out what Pan Pistryak had said to him, who also did not know how to say a comprehensible word but said whatever came into his head. But with that word he only slightly lifted his hat from his head and quickly put it back on his head, and said respectfully, looking at everyone but not looking at anyone specifically: "Greetings!" And, of course, it's like this everywhere: the more foolish the chief, the prouder he is, and know it stinks to high heaven like burning animal skins.

"Greetings, our dear noble Pan Captain!" the people bubbled, the men began to hum, the women began to scream, the children squeaked, and bowed down low to him....

Here Ryhorovych whispered in Pan Mykyta's ear:

"Taketh some action, thou will disseminate order in our Holy Land...."

"Give me a break, damn fool!" Pan Ulasovych whispered to him, "how can I disseminate, or do whatever there, when I do not understand anything about what this is."

"Thus, thou shalt not create diversion for me !" said the scribe and went off to take care of his matters.

Well, well! Although our Pan Captain, Mykyta Ulasovych, was not a wise man, he had enough common sense not to get involved in something he knew nothing about. When he did not understand the case at all, he did not become capricious about anything, unlike our Judge General, may he rest in peace! Don't think of stopping him: whether to the point or not, he would sign what was put in front of him. The scribe was about to stop him – no way! "I don't want the case to linger around," he'd say, "I'll sign it, that's the end of it!" Therefore, whenever the scribe saw that the judge was going to the collegium, he immediately hid all the papers, otherwise the judge would sign them all right away. Once – oh, there was much laughter! (I was still serving at the collegium and was learning to write syllables because I was still a boy in my nineteenth year) – the junior scribes wrote a document that said the judge should be tonsured as a monk, and his wife be given in marriage to Pan Cavalry Officer, who often went to the forest with her to gather mushrooms. Well, they laid that letter before the judge. As soon as he entered, he sat down, saw the letter, pulled it toward himself to take a closer look, crossed himself, and said: "May they not wait long! Let them thank me for making a quick decision on the case; and let the guilty man feel sorry for himself." And with a scratch of his pen, he signed "with his own hand." And the lads – ha, ha, ha, ha! The scribe smacked them hard on the backs of their heads and made them leave the room, and explaining that letter to the judge, tore it to pieces... It was all in vain. We will finish saying what we have to say.

Pan Ulasovych stood there with his hands on his hips, like the F written in a Kyivan grammar book[16] until Khoma Kalyberda, an elderly man, came up to him, and, taking off his hat, bowed to him about five times, and then dared to say:

"Thank you, Pan Ulasovych, for your love of olden times. Your deceased grandfather, Pan Opanas, may the earth lying above him be light as a feather, did not let harm come to us. Should there be a little bit of drought, right away he would go after the pagan witches; and after he gets three or four drowned, then the rain would come! And everything was all right! What times of yore! What sweetmeat!"

"That would be a bit of news that's not bad," said Pan Zabryokha, respectfully, and stepped back from Kalyberda, so that he could not trouble him too much and would not

----

[16] For the word "Farter." For an explanation of this see: http://ukrlit.org/slovnyk/%D1%85%D0%B2%D0%B5%D1%80%D1%82.

become too familiar with him by chance. In order to get away from him as soon as possible, he called out to Ryhorovych and said:

"What now?"

Catching his breath, Ryhorovych, went up to him and coughed, twitching his mustache – this was a sign that he would start spewing his Holy Writ – saying:

"'Tis time to hurry to foin and drag the unclean woman into the watery depths. Anon, come hither, my brothers, be bold!"

The Kozak guards, when they heard the scribe's command, immediately unhooked Vekla Shtyrykha from the assembly of witches; they grabbed her immediately by the arms and legs tightly so that she could not escape, and, laughing, rushed to the boats... She shouted: "Help!" Little children ran after her and wailed as if she were already dead; old Shtyrya limped after them and wept, and scolded both the Kozaks and Captain, but most of all the scribe... No one paid any attention to them, and several shouted: "Hold her tighter, Yosyp! See, she is resisting..." And another says, "Gotcha? Well? This is not like milking cows at midnight..." And many things were attached until she was brought to the boat, pulled into it, and then they held her tighter. When they brought her to the posts, they tied and twisted her arms and legs nicely; and they made a noose out of the rope that was attached to the posts, and, pulling her upward with the ropes, plunged her into the water... Like a giant stone, she sunk to the bottom, until only bubbles were gurgling!....

"Pull her back, pull!... She is not a witch, not a witch!" the people began to shout in unison, and those who were younger and standing closer rushed to help those who were near the ropes...

"Immerse her more and more, immerse the thricely damned daughter of Canaan!," roared Prokip Ryhorovych and stopped the people from pulling Vekla back.

"Listen to me," Ulasovych shouted with all his strength. "After all, I am the Captain. I give the command: pull her back! After all, she did not come back to the surface, so she's not a witch."

"She's not a witch, not a witch; she did not come back to the surface, she's not a witch; pull her back!" all the people shouted, and no one was listening to the scribe any longer, and they pulled Vekla out completely dead, unhooked her from the ropes, and, without putting her on the ground, began to pump out her lungs.

While this was going on, Pan Captain, resting up after the shouting and disturbance, called Ryhorovych over to him and asked:

"Tell me for mercy's sake: why did you command for her to be drowned? The woman is not yet old and from a rich and honorable family; she hasn't been capricious.

"I judge by righteousness and I act without any circumvention," said Ryhorovych, "although she is not yet an old woman, she has a devilish amount of money. For she did not give what I asked; she did not believe in loans; she did not pay ransom to the guards like the others. For this reason, I thought about submerging her and not taking her out until she gives me what I want and how much I am asking for. Diehard, the fig to her mother, thrice-tenaciously die-hard. I see that she's already been shaken out. Let her prosper for a time. And bring Ustya Vecherykha here!" Ryhorovych shouted at the guards.

They dragged over Ustya, and everything happened just the same as with Vekla, only as they splashed Ustya into the water, she sank right away and Amen to her! Although they shook her, they didn't pump the water out of her, and so she remained dead.

Pan Captain asked the scribe about her, the latter surreptitiously confessed: "That," he says, "I wouldst desire to fornicate with her daughter Odaria, who is quite dazzling, and she, being thrice-staunchly impious, instead of the desired maiden, put into my pocket a thousand-damned pumpkin and covered my front and back with shame, like a scab. So, this is what she gets for pulling such a prank...."

Then bowing low, Talymin Levurda interrupted them and asked:

"Be so kind, Pan Captain Ulasovych, maybe they could dunk my wife a little, because she is doing a little witchery."

"Bring her here!" thus spoke Pan Zabryokha, as if he were singing. "Don't let us catch you, we will teach you a lesson straight away, but most of all those who give good people pumpkins instead of embroidered betrothal towels." And he thought of his own misfortune, sighed heavily, bowed his head and stood there.

On hearing about what Levurda requested, Prokip Ryhorovych began to shake, like a gypsy in the cold; his eyes began to sparkle, his face turned red, his lips began to tremble, and he could just barely say a word:

"How do ye.. And for what do ye want... to drown your wife?... Is she doing sorcery?"

"How is she not doing sorcery?" Talymin Levurda told Ulasovych. "Listen here, my good man! About ten times I have had a dream that in the very darkest midnight someone knocked on the my window; knocked and knocked, until my Stekha, you know, my wife, wakes up. She wakes up and steps out of the house, and I fall asleep, and before dawn she returns. So I ask, "Where have you, I say, been?" And she says, "I went out to the cows and I got frozen, so I will lie down." And I say: "Lie down," and she lies down and says, "I'm frozen," but she herself is hot as a fire. So, you see, my good man, she did not go to the cows, but to conjure, probably, to conjure. And then on that Sunday, I saw the devil most alive as I now see you, Pan Captain, may you be healthy. You see: I went to the market fair and had to stay there for three days, but I got sick, and I returned late at night on the same day. Knock-knock on the door to the house – my wife does not come out and is talking to someone and laughing boisterously, and there is a light on. As I yanked the door, the latch came unstuck and I entered. I looked... it's the devil visiting her, but, as you can see, exactimally like Pan Scribe Prokip Ryhorovych, may he be healthy. The same mug, and clothing, and everything else. I go up to him, but he moves away from me. I go after him, and the damned devil goes into the loft area (and I closed the loft door). He sees that he's in a pickle and jumps into a stovepipe. I am frightened when I return to the house and clamber onto the plank bed above the stove. What a discovery. I covered myself with a pelt, and I shuddered with fright that I had seen the devil, and my wife is friends with him. So, I say to you: my wife is suspicious, completely suspicious, douse her at least a little, then maybe it will rain.

"Why not? So, we'll douse her. Pan Scribe, well then!" Pan Captain said to Ryhorovych. The latter shouts back at him with his all might!

"Have you gone mad?" He shouted at him. "Have you simply gone crazy?" You will not be allowed to make any decision without my calling for it, because it is necessary to finalize the whole matter and legally unify the subjoining. And you, devilish Levurda! this is what the law commands you to do. The holy spirit is with you, Pan Ulasovych – we ought to put this so-and-so's legs in the stocks – that wretched Talymon Levurda, who by his delusion led his poor wife to friendship with Satan. Hey, lads! Grab him and take him to the town hall and put his feet in the stocks, for he has consciously confessed that he has seen a living devil; for he is a sorcerer, a wizard. In the morning I will beat this sinner with cudgels."

While Pistryak was relating this, and the poor wretch Levurda was already being rushed to the town hall, and Ryhorovych looked up and exchanged glances with some black-haired young woman, smiled, twitched his moustache, and shouted at the Kozak guards: "Well then, plunge Domakha Karlyuchkivna into the watery underworld!" The pond only gurgled after Karlyuchkivna was tied in it ... And the people, seeing that she was not floating to the surface, shouted: "No, she was not a witch, she was not!"

And Priska Chyryachka, Khymka Ryabokobylykha, and Pazka Psyuchykha were tossed in the water to be drowned. Some were revived and some were taken away. So, the people pounded the ground in frustration, wondering: "Where is there a witch here? Each one was tossed into the water and each one sank, and no witch could be found among them." Mykyta Ulasovych had already begun to doze off. In his opinion, it was time to go home: whether it rained or not, he didn't care much. If he was out of bread, they would bring him some: Konotop is not a small village; you won't get by without quarreling and litigation.

Gaping and looking at our Pistryak, who became pensive and tapped his brow with his finger, then his nose, he thought for a while and shouted: "Let us see the last of the pagans. Bring Yavdokha Zubykha here!" They brought that one, pushing the boat up to the pilings, tied her up with ropes, raised her up... plop! Our Yavdokha hit the water like a board, and did not submerge, but floated like a fish on top of the water. She lay there, and moving her tied hands and feet, tilting her belly and lower back, she chanted: "Swimming-swimmie-swimmie-swim!"

All the people were so horrified! "She's a witch, yes, yes!" they all cried out. And as Mykyta Ulasovych yawned and saw this wonder, his mouth was left agape; and Prokip Ryhorovych was nearly dancing on the bank and shouting at the workers: "Pull her up again! Toss her into the water's darkness!" So what? No matter how much he shouted, he could do nothing to Yavdokha. They pulled her up, heaved her with all their strength into the water...over and over she did not sink and even mocked everyone, striking the water: "Kupochky-kuponky."

"Bring over stones and bricks!" ordered Pan Pistryak, coming up with a new idea. Thus an entire pile of bricks and stones of all kinds emerged that the lads, hearing the order, immediately rolled and carried over.

"Lay the stones on her unholy neck, and on her arms, and on her feet, and drown her," so commanded Ryhorovych, practically jumping around the circle of the pond, gnashing his teeth from anger.

They hurriedly tied an entire string of stones on the rope and rowed it over on the boats. Three men could barely lift the string of stones and threw it over Yavdokha Zubykha's neck and thought: she'll drown! And she, demonic woman, would not drown; she just floated on top of the water. They released her hand from the rope, so she waved it, and joked: "What of it? You attached a nice necklace to my neck, but there are no rings? Hee hee! See how good you are! You'd better put rings on my fingers and shoes on my feet instead of that."

"Crush the thrice-cursed Canaanite sorceress, the Chaldean daughter!" Prokip Ryhorovych shouted as if he had been burned, and he foamed at the mouth like a madman, seeing that he could not do anything to the witch and that she was mocking him.

They put the stones on her hands and feet – the man who told me about it swore as much. If you know, Iokhym Khvaida, who died more than a year ago, he vowed that about twenty poods [320 pounds] were tied to her neck, arms, and legs, and, unhooking her from the ropes, they lowered her into the water... So, what are you going to do with this shrew of a wench? So, she floats on top of the water, and dangles with her hands and feet and says: "Kupochky-kupusi" And then the demonic wench turned to the scribe and began to call to him: "Come here, Prokip honey! Let's go swimming together. Come on, don't be shy! I will place a necklace on you and I will give you rings..." And Ryhorovych ripped out his entire scalplock out of anger that the evil wench would mock him; then he rushed to Ulasovych and said:

"Undoubtedly, this wench comes from among the Egyptian Babi[17]. She is a vicious viper. She purloined the rain drops and secreted them in her own old tub or in a different place. Pan Captain, order them to give her a good thrashing so that she suffers unbearably and releases the watery splashes, and the earth will become covered in droplets."

"Pan Scribe, I do not comprehend what you are saying; and I say to you, do what you want, just more quickly, because it's time for lunch. I would have left a long time ago. I am so fed up with this comedy --there is an entire cart of stones on this hag, and yet she does not sink, but floats on top of the water. Do what you want, and I will look at the result. That is why I am the captain in Konotop.

Ryhorovych ordered them to capture Yavdokha in the water. But no such luck! The lads could not catch up to her in their boats, and they threw ropes at her, but nothing happened. She was swimming as fast as a pike, the waves rising only in front and behind her, because, of course, she swims like a witch: not the way we do! She swam and swam, and kept scurrying around, but as soon as she saw that she had tired everyone out, she succumbed....

Well, the people rejoiced as Yavdokha Zubykha the witch was caught! Everyone shouted, created a stir, ran up to her from all sides. Everybody wanted to give her a shove or a smack in the back of the head... Yes, and there is reason to do

....

[17] Babi or Baba is an Egyptian god of the underworld and a guardian of the deceased. He is depicted as an aggressive and ferocious baboon god. His name Baba is similar to the Ukrainian word *baba*, which can be used pejoratively and translated as "wench." The word *baba* also is the standard word for grandmother in Ukrainian.

that! Let her not steal clouds from the sky, nor hide the rain in the cupboard... Even as everyone was running around her, then behind her, they carried her in their arms, fearing lest she escape and flee, yet she did not care! She sang a wedding song, the way a young bride walks with her maids of honor. And our Ryhorovych led in front and even ran with joy because he had gotten the witch, and he would now pinch and torment her, so that she would give back the rain that she has stolen, and out of joy he was talking such nonsense, that no one, not even he could make out for himself what he was saying. Then he cried out, "And ye shall taketh now the willow switches, and double up the vines, and mocketh her, whilst thou hast your strength."

They found cut willow branches. They tied up Yavdokha Zubykha. As soon as she had been lain down, she somehow stuck out her hand and motioned it in a circle around the people. Now, listen to what came of this. So, they laid her down; two young lads sat on her legs and feet, and two took hefty bundles of willow and began to thrash her. Swish-swish! Swish-swish! They were practicaly out of breath! They beat and kept beating her and already the broken branches were flying... But what about Yavdokha? Lying under the cut switches, she relates a fairytale: "There once was a man Sazhka, he was wearing a gray, felt cap and a patch on his back; do you wanna listen to my good fairytale again?"

"Beat the accursed Canaanite!" Pistryak roared.

The lads beat her up as much as they could, but Yavdokha said, "And you say, 'Beat the accursed Cunaanite,' and I say, "There once was a man Sazhka, he was wearing a gray, felt cap, and a patch on his back; do you wanna listen to my good fairytale again?"

"Yes, beat her harder!" Pan Konotop Captain, Mykyta Ulasovych Zabryokha, shouted himself. He was already feeling very sick to his stomach as if his liver was about to explode, because he had not eaten anything yet.

The lads swapped places, took the bundles, and began to flog her, but Zubykha started up again: "And you say, 'Beat harder' and I say, 'Beat harder'; 'There once was a man Sazhka, he was wearing a gray, felt cap, and a patch on his back; do you wanna listen to my good fairytale again?'"

"Take the thorny twigs and double the thrashing on her lewd groin!" Pan Pistryak commanded, thinking for a long time what else he could come up with to do to her.

The lads beat Yavdokha with the thorny twigs, but Yavdokha beat back with: "And you say: Take the thorny twigs and double the thrashing of her lewd groin and I say: Take the thorny twigs and double the thrashing of her lewd groin. There once was a man Sazhka, he was wearing a gray, felt cap, and a patch on his back; do you wanna listen to my good fairytale again?...."

And you would not be able to relate everything that happened there until the evening! No longer just Ryhor-ovych Pistryak, but also Captain Zabryokha himself began to get angry that there was no end to the venture. They kept on beating the demonic wench, how many lads had taken shifts, how many twigs had been tried: willow, birch, and thorns. And nothing affected her, as if she had only laid down and was not being beaten at all, but she just kept nattering about this guy Sazhka....

So, while all this was happening, and they beat the viper-like, Catholic[18] Yavdokha, the people clustered all around Yavdokha and couldn't stop wondering, the old and hesitant man, Demko Shvandyura, stepped up. He watched for a while, shook his head, and said:

....

[18]   The Kozaks were Orthodox Christians and considered Catholics (both Roman Catholic Poles and Uniate Ukrainian Greek Catholics) enemies.

   HRYHORIY KVITKA-OSNOVYANENKO

"What kind of a game is this! Or has Pan Captain become bored, so you amuse him like a little child, as if you were thrashing a willow log like someone important?"

"Like a log? What is he saying? Who is beating a log?" the people begin to raise a ruckus and ask in surprise.

"Where is the log? Don't you see it? Look!" Schvandyura said, and waved his hand over the people counterclockwise... So, what? What a surprise! Then they all saw that a thick willow log was lying there, wrapped with ropes, and four hefty lads were sitting on it and holding it as well as they could so that it would not resist, and the four of them were beating that log with all their strength with good cuttings of branches, as if it were someone important. And next to that log Yavdokha Zubykha was lying unbound, and laughing boisterously, watching how the people were working on the log instead of her. So, will you tell me that this wasn't a marvel? Thus, as she had been placed there for thrashing, she waved her hand and let an illusion fall on everyone there, and Demko came with fresh eyes and saw what was happening, since he knew a thing or two and was able to do something against it, then he removed the spell from the people. Only then could they see that they were not beating Yavdokha, but a log from a willow tree.

"Ha, ha, ha, ha!..,," the people started laughing boisterously. Even though Pan Scribe had gotten really angry, he himself burst into laughter when he saw such a comedy. And what are you going to do? Obviously, you won't do anything against the spell if you do not know how to avert it. Well, after having laughed a bit, they started to figure out what to do with Yavdokha. They said all kinds of things, but Demko Schvandyura, taught them well:

"Well," he says, "don't think of anything else, having put her down, now keep giving her a good whipping until the rain and dew return, which, I know, are sitting on the shelf in her cupboards. But do not be fearful of anything. She will not be able to cast another spell in my presence. If she does, I will remove it. Although she's a witch, we still know something, although not everything. Let her skill be by birth and mine acquired, never mind! We will see!"

"So, get her once again!" – cried Ryhorovych, "and give her a good whipping, the kind in olden days they made for Saturday punishments at school...." He barely finished his command, and the lads already started up: they pulled off her clothes, laid her down, and started beating her... and our Yavdokha was no longer up to telling a fairytale; she already had on her back... about seventy patches, like that man Sazhka... She was silent for a long time, she wanted to endure it without moaning... The person has not been born yet to endure that many switches! And then she whined and wailed... and began to shout: "I will not do it again in my life!... please, my dear lads!.. Let me go, let me go!.. I will return the rain, and return the dew... I will be at your service, Pan Captain… and yours, Ryhorovych... just let me go...."

"Enough," Mykyta Ulasovych said in a respectful voice. And Pistryak said what he had to say:

"Do it more and more!

The lads did not know whom to listen to: half of them kept beating her, and the others just waited.

"To hell with you, Pan Captain!" Pan Ryhorovych growled at him. "It should be done five times more for such a misdeed... She bewitched me so that after drinking I was delirious. Such a misdeed ....

"Well—a misdeed!" Pan Zabryokha said, "you can't think of anything but misdeeds. We are just wasting time here, and it's time to have lunch. Who knows if it will rain or not after such a thrashing, but it is utterly certain that we are starving. And what disgrace can the bitch cause us out of rage, so should we be afraid? We should just leave Yavdokha. Let her rest after such a bath. Let's do nothing for now, we will get around to her later. Let's go to my house, Prokip Ryhorovych. Pazka cooked some delicious borscht. And afterward I will not take a nap but will tell you how I was disgraced the day before yesterday at Bezverkhy Khutir. You don't know about it yet. Having said this, Pan Ulasovych dragged himself home. Our Prokip Ryhorovych stayed and stood there as if he had been scalded. He was occupied by his thoughts and surmises about what kind of disgrace Pan Captain suffered at Bezverkhy Khutir. He kept on thinking, meanwhile Yavdokha was being thrashed so hard that the twigs were flying! Then he put his finger up and said, "I figured it out! heh, heh, heh! This is what I wanted! And lads, let this poor old wench no longer be tortured in vain. Pan Captain ordered her to be whipped until the evening, but I will have mercy on her."

They raised Yavdokha and dragged her home barely alive. The people made such a fuss over her, everyone shouted: "She's a witch, a witch! She stole the rain from the heavens!" And Ryhorovych walked along and contemplated, saying: "This is what I wanted!... I will entice her with gifts, and she will help me ruin him. Then they will promote me from my scribe's position to a lordship..." And he went off to Pan Mykyta Ulasovych's to dine.

VI

The sad and unhappy Yavdokha Zubykha, the witch of Konotop, wandered around her house after being publicly thrashed at the pond for practicing sorcery. She had just seen someone off and closed the door behind him. But who would have come to her when everyone shunned her for being a natural born witch who would not drown in water with stones tied to her, who stole rain from the sky, and caused harm to people with her spells. Who? None other than our dear Prokip Ryhorovych Pistryak, the scribe of Konotop. Upon hearing from Captain Ulasovych about the special treatment he had received from Pannochka[19] Olena at Bezverkhy Khutir, he immediately devised a plot to get rid of the captain entirely. Prokip came to Yavdokha's house in the afternoon, bringing her various gifts and pretending to reconcile with her. He made it seem that it had been Captain Ulasovych's idea rather than his to drown her and then thrash her until the evening, though he had taken it up himself. Then the scribe asked her earnestly to make a fool of that Pan Mykyta when he came to her that evening and pleaded for her to use her magic to make Olena Yosypovna fall in love with and marry him. As soon as Ulasovych succumbed to the sorcery, he would go crazy and step down from his position which he, Pistryak, would take over and

....

[19]   An endearing for a young unmarried Ukrainian girl – something like Sweet Miss or Missy Olena.

he promised her that then she would be free to practice her witchcraft to her heart's content.

Cunning Yavdokha seemingly fell for Prokip's ploy. She accepted his gifts and assured him she would do as he asked. After seeing him off from her house, she kept pondering something, feeling uneasy and unsettled. She would have been happy to take a seat, but it was impossible – so sincere was that righteous thrashing. She tried lying on the stove-top-bed and on the bench, but only for a short while. She could only lie on her stomach but could not rest on her back or side – she was sore all over.

The witch kept walking around her house, looking at the jugs, pots, and mugs where she stored milk from all sorts of beasts and reptiles. She would carefully approach each creature under a different guise so that they wouldn't be frightened and let her milk them. All these vessels were sitting on the shelf or in the cupboard, some were on the hearth, and others on the stove. Some contained cream already, while others were placed under the bench and near the washbasin.

She kept various herbs and roots under the floorboards, including mint, lovage, agrimony, fern, dog's mercury, thornapple, all kinds of burdocks, monkswort – you name it. A striped and whiskered tomcat was lounging on a cushion on the floor. The cat's only business was to eat and sleep and, when something crossed his mind, he would immediately communicate it to his mistress with a "meow." She would smile and reply....

"Here, kitty kitty, here!" And when something crossed her mind, she would ask him, "Am I right, kitty?" And he would respond to her, "Meow, meow!" Oh, they really did understand each other's language. She didn't have much of a household, but why would she need more? Should she desire something, at night she would turn into a dog, mouse, frog, or fish and get it. She always had what she needed.

Feeling sad, she walked about her house and, looking at her collection, said to herself, "There's everything I need. I won't go borrowing from people." Then she glanced at the door, which – as I mentioned – she had just closed, having seen someone off, and she said, "Hurry up and bring that damned captain, and I will pay him back. I'd rather give you a good thrashing, too, Ryhorovych, but I'll leave that for later. For now, you serve me, and once I've eaten up that scoundrel Zabryokha, I'll get you Pistryak, you son of a bitch! It's good that you told me about Zabryokha and Olena: I'll marry him off... you'll also get what you deserve for torturing me so badly, to the point where I can't even sit or lie down. I'll get even with you for ridiculing me and tearing my *plakhta* (skirt) and my long shirt in front of the young men, for uncovering my hair, for thrashing me, oh, for beating me! They beat and beat and kept on beating me! It hurts so much that I can neither sit nor lie down; it's all that damned Shvandyura's fault. He removed my spell."

And thus she kept talking to herself for a long while until it became completely dark in the house, so dark that she could barely see... Then suddenly the dogs barked outside, and she said, "Come on, kitty, open your eyes and shine so that I can see if they are coming." The cat opened his eyes and glared. They sparkled like fire, and Yavdokha saw that Mykyta Ulasovych Zabryokha, the Captain from Konotop, was coming, followed by his scribe, Prokip Ryhorovych Pistryak. They were carrying some things in their hands and under their arms. Immediately, she darted over, took an oil lamp, rubbed it against the cat's fur so that sparks flew from it and lit the lamp. She placed the lamp on the table and crawled under the table to retrieve something.

Suddenly, the door opened, and in walked Pan Captain accompanied by the scribe. They placed their hats and canes near the door and started looking around. Captain Zabryokha spoke up, "The light is on, but it seems she's not at home."

"Where could I be then!" retorted Zubykha, emerging from under the table in the corner and dragging a large pot topped with a piece of cloth. "That's where I was. I've brought out this pot of clouds that I had hidden for an eternity since the Konotop captain forced me to release the clouds and bring forth rain."

"Well, dear, let's forget about that," bowed Captain Zabryokha and began taking out gifts. "Here's a kerchief that a priest's daughter embroidered and gave me as a gift. I offer it to you as a token of my respect, and here's a whole heap of money as well. Please, auntie, don't be angry with me and forgive me for what had to happen to you... It's like, that is, I kind of... really didn't mean to...."

"What do you mean, you didn't mean to?" screamed Yavdokha, "You didn't mean to? If someone had smashed your kisser the same way... you would sing a different tune. I don't want your gifts, shame on you! Go to hell! May your gifts be cursed! Don't bother me. I'm going to release the rain; otherwise, I will be punished again, and tomorrow they'll give me another thrashing. I am not able to sit down today, and tomorrow I won't even be able to stand. Let me go, and I'll go release the rain."

"Dear auntie, dear!" Poor Mykyta Ulasovych fell to his knees, kissing the bony hands of the witch and pleading. "I won't bother you anymore, and what do I care if there's no rain? Why should I! I'm the Captain here, I won't starve. There is always someone coming with bread, another with *palyanytsya*[20], another with a loaf, and another with a little bag of flour. As long as they keep coming, those of us in power do not care about rain, even if you, auntie, kept it hidden in your corner under the table forever. Help me in

....

[20] A Ukrainian baked rustic rye or wheat bread: https://www.kitchenepiphanies.com/palianytsia-rustic-bread-ukraine/.

my plight! Here, please take these: a bottle of pear liqueur, fifty or so smoked fish, still fresh from spring: and here's a little *serpanok* (headscarf)... just do me a favor, help me in my need, here's what I'll tell you..."

"Oh, I am perfectly aware of your troubles. I know what a well-roasted pumpkin you received from Olena, Yosyp's daughter from Bezverkhy Khutir, and how you barely came back to your senses on the second day! I'm well aware, indeed.

Even Pan Zabryokha was taken aback, wondering how she seemed to know it all, as if she had been right there, and he started pleading more zealously, hoping she wouldn't stay mad and would vouch for him.

"And how can I help you?" Yavdokha inquired. "If the cornet's daughter won't marry you, then what can I do about it? If she won't have you, then seek another."

"But where the hell am I to find another like her?" gasped Ulasovych. "Firstly, I can't even figure out where to find someone else, and secondly, I don't want anyone else because I've fallen head over heels for Olena Yosypovna. Even if the daughters of judges or colonels should come my way, I would not give them a second glance, for I've fallen for Olena with my whole being – my body, soul, heart, and every ounce of me. And I see it clearly, if I don't attain her, I'll either drown myself or hang myself, or go off wherever my feet will carry my... Help me, dearie!" he exclaimed, falling at her feet and even shedding tears, begging her not to let him perish by his own hand, and imploring her to enchant the girl somehow so that she'd be willing to marry him.

"But how can a girl like her marry you?" Yavdokha replied skeptically. "She's a fine lass. In her attire and her looks, she's got it all – cattle and money—and you? Where do you fit in?"

"But never mind that, auntie, dear mother, never mind! Let me be ugly and repulsive, let me be anything; but you must make it so that she loves me and wants to marry me.

Here is a pile of money for you on the table. Here's forty altyns, and...."

"No," Yavdokha said, pushing the money away. "I don't need these trinkets. What use are they to me? I have everything I want, and I can get whatever I desire. But if you're begging so earnestly, then maybe I'll take pity on you, just do me a favor...."

"Whatever you ask, dear lady, I'll do it all. If you want me to burn down Konotop, I will set it all on fire; or you want to do away with the entire Konotop youth – those darned rascals you don't like – I will smash them all to bits in a single day...."

"And that's all well and good, dearie, but now listen what I truly desire. Put that wretched son of a bitch Shvandyura under arrest. He removed the spell I placed on the people and then they gave me a really hard time. So, arrest him on the grounds of stealing something or insulting you or whatever you can come up with to frame him, and milk him dry. Fine him and take away his cattle. Because he's quite well-off, you know! And make sure his relatives don't come knocking on your door, so hand over all of that to Pan Scribe Ryhorovych....

"A good deed and wise decision, Pani Zubykha, oh yes indeed!" chimed in Pan Pistryak, lounging by the window. And Yavdokha went on: "He's got nowhere else to turn, poor thing, just feeding off inheritances. Kick Schvandyura out of the village, so he doesn't stink up the place. Once you do that for me, I'll return the favor...."

"Purr, meow, purr!" the witch's cat interjected, and it suddenly occurred to Zubykha: "Oh, no, wait, there's another thing. That Domashyn's daughter-in-law Khvenna Zozulykha... I can't even approach her house, because she accused me of stealing a bed sheet from her garden, the one that somehow ended up in my chest. She calls me a thief and blabs to everyone. Can't we kick her out of the village too, by any chance?"

"Why not? Just say the word, I'll do it all..." said Pan Ulasovych, delighted that the witch was being more agreeable.

"As long as you do all that, I'll..."

"Purr, purr!" the cat purred again, and Zubykha started bargaining again, saying: "And there's one more thing I'd like to complain about. Demko Siroshtan won't leave me in peace. The day before yesterday, he boasted he'd kill my cat if I didn't watch over it carefully, and he'll actually do it. So, you, Captain, should give him a good lesson..."

"Oh, I'll teach him a lesson, auntie! He will smarten up and never forget it. Just do what I ask you..." pleaded Captain Zabryokha, leaning in earnestly, willing to promise her anything if she'd just start things rolling and get the cornet's daughter to marry him.

"All right, my boy, if that's the way it is, then so be it. The cornet's daughter Olena won't get a wink of sleep at night and will be running after you just like you are running after her. Kitty, kitty, kitty, kitty.

"Purr, purr, meow, purr, meow!"

"Very well," Yavdokha said. "Now, Pan Ulasovych, come with me outside, step onto the sand with your left foot, so your mark will be etched into the sand."

So, she led him out of the house, gathered his footprint in her handkerchief, and tied it up. Then, returning to the house, she seated him on a bench at the table's edge, instructed Ryhorovych to light the oil-lamp, and grabbing Pan Zabryokha by his left mustache, she began to separate strands of hair. She separated a hair with her fingernail and counted, "One, two, three..." Just as she got to the ninth one, she snapped it... The captain yelled, and the scribe burst into laughter... Yavdokha Zubykha whispered something and spat, while the cat purred throughout the house... And that's how poor Mykyta Ulasovych lost the ninth hair from his left mustache, and the witch plucked out all the other eight of them, took a piece of paper and wrapped the hair inside. And wiping away the tears that were streaming from the plucking, Pan Zabryokha began to ask the witch, "If you're done, can I go?" he said.

"Go in peace, my son, go home and get some rest. Wait for a message from the cornet's daughter Olena to send for the embroidered wedding cloths."

Upon hearing this, Pan Ulasovych hastily put on his hat, dashed out of the house, and not even glancing back, he headed straight home, lest the witch should feel like plucking out more hair. Poor thing. He ran, quite agitated, not waiting for his scribe, who was still back at the witch's place, engaged in a lengthy conversation, with the cat purring alongside them. As Pan Pistryak exited Yavdokha's house, you could hear him saying:

"And having sorted everything out so nobly, I'm off to my Promised Land. Farewell!"

"Go in good health!" Yavdokha said, closing the door behind him, and called out to the cat: "Kitty, kitty, kitty, kitty!"

"Purr, meow, purrrr!"

And right away she took her head cover off, let down her milky-colored gray hair, put on a white shirt without a belt or a *plakhta* (skirt), and just wandered around the house, muttering all sorts of spells and spitting three times in every corner. Then she took a *zhlukto* (washtub) and placed it in the middle of the room and started mumbling something witchy again. Then she took some water from a jug, mumbling all the while, and sprinkled herself and inside the *zhlukto* with that water... All the while the cat was meowing with its all might. He even stood on his hind legs and widened his eyes, shining even brighter than the oil lamp in the room... So, Yavdokha swiftly started climbing into the *zhlukto*.. and once inside she turned into a maiden! And the maiden wasn't a simpleton! She was young, beautiful, and raven-haired, probably even more gorgeous than the priest's daughter from Chernihiv!

Just as our witch transformed, she took some frog's sour cream and horse's cheese, some smoked fish heads, and after placing it all on a little plate, she set it in front of her cat and said: "My kitty, if you feel like eating without me, then here are some treats for you. Don't miss me too much while I'm gone." And taking as many as five containers for milk, she extinguished the oil-lamp and left the house to milk whatever she needed to.

But just as the second rooster crowed, as quickly as she could, Yavdokha rushed back into the house and collapsed as if she were lifeless. And when she caught her breath and got up... she had turned into an old woman again, just as she was before. Right away, she ran up to her cat and started talking to him as if he were a man: "Kitty, my little one! Did you miss me at all? It took me a little longer: after milking all the cows and sheep, I still needed to get some pike's milk for one thing. I dashed to the pond, but it took a while to calm the darn pike down, and then to negotiate with her to let me milk her when the first rooster crowed. Though it posed no danger to us, I still had to hurry so that the second rooster wouldn't crow. Otherwise, I'd be stretched out right on the street, just like I am here now...."

And the cat wagged his tail knowingly, blinked his eyes, and kept meowing. He was really delighted that his mistress had returned.

And so, she placed all kinds of milk and cream in front of him, and started bustling about, mixing and brewing her magic, until finally, it was dawn! But then a little later, a woman came to her, her head all wrapped up, and she was sighing. Then she entered, and she sighed, and she sat down, and she kept sighing.

"Where are you from, young lady?" Yavdokha asked her.

"From quite a distance away!" the young woman exclaimed, catching her breath. "Do you happen to know the farmstead on Sukha Balka by the name of Bezverkhy... oh!"

Yavdokha winked at the cat and said, "No, I've never heard of it, never been there, and I don't know who lives there... Why did you come to me then?"

"Well, not to put it lightly, I caught cellulitis and now my face is swollen ... oh! So, the townsfolk sent me to you... Please, auntie, do whatever you can, just help me so I can make it to our cornet's daughter, Pannochka Olena Yosypovna, today." As she spoke, she placed a loaf of bread, five eggs, and a small pile of coins on the table.

Zubykha immediately sprang into action, placed her blade down, and instructed the young woman to stand on it with her bare foot on the same side where the her cheek was swollen the worst. She fetched a coal ember from the stove and added a piece of a candle that had been blessed, a bit of frankincense, and a scrap of the same cloth they use for wrapping the Easter bread for blessing into the ember pot. She wrapped and covered the young woman, making sure all the smoke stayed focused on her, and then she whispered and spat, blowing on the ember, while the cat meowed loudly throughout the house. Smoke filled the air and suddenly the young woman collapsed onto the floor, as if lifeless. Zubykha revived her and seated her on a bench, saying, "Don't worry now, it'll pass, you will get well in no time. It's an evil eye; some dark-haired lad gazed at you and envied you...."

"That's right! It's our young master," the young woman said. "Whenever he sees me, he's certainly stealing glances at me. Last week he even reached out and caressed my cheek with his hand, saying, 'Damn, what a beautiful young lady!' I blushed in embarrassment, and ever since then, I've been in this state...."

Then Yavdokha began questioning her about what she needed... and eventually escorted her out of the house, saying, "Now it's good! Now I know everything I need..."

VII

The sad and unhappy, Pannochka Olena Yosypovna, the cornet ́s daughter, sat on the porch of her house at Bezverhy Khutir on Sukha Balka. Her white hands were idly playing with her brother ́s, the cornet ́s son's, hair. That day, the poor thing had lunch with the priest, who had come to visit him, having buried someone at another farmstead. After eating a hefty lot of dumplings and crucian carp fried in sour cream and washing the lunch down with buttermilk (for this was already happening after St. Peter ́s Day[21]), they downed a whole pitcher of thornbush liquor between the two of them and chased it down with cherry brandy for the road. And in the afternoon, the lad treated himself to as many as five round cheese curd pancakes and a small pot of mushrooms fried in butter and sour cream, which he dearly loved. For no apparent reason, he felt a bit too full to the point that it bothered him. And so, he placed his head on his sister ́s lap and fell asleep as she was running her fingers through his hair. Then the cows and sheep came from the field; they were milked near her, and the milk was poured into pots... but she was indifferent! As if she had no concern for anything! She forgot to watch over the milking, she forgot to pet her younger brother ́s hair, her mind was preoccupied with only one thought...

....

[21] On July 12 according to the Julian calendar and on June 30 according to the Gregorian.

Just as I was about to tell you what our cornet́s daughter was thinking and why she was sad and unhappy, suddenly she was approached by an old granny, so very old that she seemed to be barely holding herself upright. She came up to her and said:

"Good evening to you, young lady! May God help you!"

Yosypovna flinched, since she hadn't seen where the woman came from and how she appeared before her. Then, having recovered her senses, the girl said: "Greetings, Granny! And whence did God bring you?"

"Oh, I just... I'm from far away and not from afar, I'm from here and not from here at all; I know nothing and I know everything; I know and I don't know who's sad and what they are sad about; and I know and I don't know what to do,..."

"Oh, Granny, are you not an ordinary person?" Olena asked.

"Oh, quite ordinary, you see! Not of your noble lineage, just a simple old woman.I don't know anyone's sorrow, I don't know who sits on the porch and longs for Demyan who went on the campaign with the Kozaks. I also don't know who spent the whole night with him by the well and, as a farewell token, took a silver ring from his hand and gave him a handkerchief, which she herself embroidered with various silk threads..."

"Oh, I'm in a pickle, Granny! But how do you know everything?... Don't make a fuss, please, my little brother will wake up and hear, and he'll tease me... Let's wait until after dinner, then I'll call you, and you can stay the night with me, and we'll have a chat!"

"Under a full moon like this, it's time to do what needs to be done, my dear. Have your brother wake up and go to his room, I'll tell you what needs to be done, and let's get things moving. I rushed to you from Kyiv after evening prayers...."

"How is that possible? All the way from Kyiv? After evening prayers? That's simply impossible!" Olena exclaimed, bewildered. "How can you possibly leave Kyiv and arrive so quickly? Isn't it a world away?"

"Well, of course you can't walk here, but we know how it's done. Just wake up your brother sooner. Let him get to his work. I need to hurry."

"Something is troubling my brother. He seems a bit out of sorts. He was perfectly healthy, but when that young dark-haired woman who tends to the cows looked into his eyes and smiled, I saw it myself. He felt a sudden pain in his belly. Could it be an upset stomach, God forbid? Or something else?"

"It's all evil eyes. Those eyes have caused all the trouble. But don't worry, I'll sort it out. Wake up your brother, and I'll have a talk with the young woman and straighten things out. It's all her fault, she'd better back off."

Olena started to wake her brother, whose snoring echoed throughout the yard, while the granny approached the young woman... and she immediately exclaimed: "Oh, Auntie! You've come to us too?..."

"My word! Just don't shout so loud," said the granny, "now listen carefully: take... shhhh- shhhh-shhhh... It was impossible to make out what the granny was whispering to her, but later the young woman said: "All right, all right; just keep the young lady busy."

"Oh well," said the granny, "that's my business now. Come along with me." She led the young girl to Pannochka Olena and said: "I've taught this young woman how to cure your brother from an upset stomach. Follow her, my little gentleman, she'll do for you what I instructed her to. But hurry up, or your upset stomach will make you climb the wall."

"Oh, my goodness!" exclaimed the cornet's daughter, taken aback. "Go, my little brother, go quickly. Do what granny said, Motrya. But be careful, don't rush into it...."

So, the cornet's son followed the young woman into the house, and the granny – plop! – sat down near Pannochka

Olena and said: "You're yearning for your little gray dove, huh? But he's not around here, he's gone far, far away, all the way to Chernihiv…."

"How do you know all this, granny? Who told you that I'm… whether I'm yearning, or… whatever… I don't even know!" Yosypovna asked, blushing crimson.

"Well, why shouldn't I know!" replied the granny. "What are stars for if we don't gaze upon them? I'll take a look in the evening, I'll take a look at midnight. I'll take a look before dawn. And I'll know what's happening everywhere."

"If you know everything that's happening everywhere, then tell me, granny, what is he up to now…," said Olena, blushing like a crimson rose, while her tongue became as tangled as a ball of yarn.

And the granny interrupted her and said:

"Demyan?"

"Ye-ye-ye-yes!"

"Khalyavsky[22], the judge's son, Omelyanovych?"

"Precisely!"

"Well, listen, my daughter, here's what he's doing: he was with the Kozaks on parade before the Colonel. He got tired, came home, undressed, sprawled out, and went to bed, moping about you and worrying that he won't see you anytime soon."

"And they say they won't be released soon!"

"Don't worry; maybe you'll see him tonight…."

"Come on, Granny, there is no chance of my seeing him, not even tonight. He's not a bird who can fly right to me!"

"Even though he's not a bird, he might just fly over and land right in front of you, like I did. Would you like him to fly over?"

22   His last name has a range of meanings from the literal Bootleg to the figurative Nothing.

"I can't wait to see him! My nerves are all jumpy just thinking about seeing him. Please, let him fly over to me... would that cause him any harm?"

"Oh, absolutely not; he's a Kozak after all."

"Then call him, mother dear, even if just for a bit, even for an hour. I just want to catch a glimpse of him! Do whatever you know how to do, and I will generously repay you. Everything here is mine. I'll give you anything you desire."

"All right then, my dear, all right. Let's get to the tasks at hand." So, they entered the living room and locked the doors and windows since the sun was already beginning to set. The *pannochka* kindled the stove and went to fetch water, following the granny's advice: not taking a direct path to the well, but circling counterclockwise. She reached it, filled the bucket with water, and poured it onto the sun's path; she repeated the process twice more, pouring the water toward the setting sun. And as she carried the water back, she poured water into the porridge pot; and granny took herbs from her apron: lovage, motherwort, black hellebore, fern blossoms, cowslip, and tossed a little bit of everything into the porridge pot, placing it over the fire. Then, she took wheat flour, mixed it with water, and fetched a scrap of paper with a cat's brain from her pouch, plucked a bit with her finger, and placed it into the dough. Then she reached into her scarf, where she had the piece of Pan Zabryokha's footprint and divided it in half, put one of the halves into the same dough, kneaded it all together, and patted out a cake. She put it in the oven to bake, all the while muttering and mumbling incantations, instructing the cornet's daughter to sit on the floor, tucking her feet under herself, not to be scared, to be fearless no matter what she might see, and to think only of her sweetheart.

As the cake was baked, she fed it to Olena in three servings, washing it down with water that she had charmed. Then the water with herbs started to boil. Calling out to Yosypovna not to be scared, the granny took the other piece of Ulasovych's footprint and tossed it into the boiling pot, stirring vigorously. She herself practically disappeared into the oven, shouting: "Cowslip, cowslip! Bring in ten with a sip, and from ten nine, from nine eight, from eight seven, from seven six, from six five, from five four, from four three, from three two, from two one, and the good one let it be." Then, she whispered secretly so that the cornet's daughter couldn't hear: "Bring Konotop Captain Zabryokha, Mykyta Ulasovych here; and the one who's waiting and anticipating, let her drift into a slumber alleviating." And she blew a breath at Olena, who ended up dozing off, whether it was from the spell or exhaustion.

And again, the old malevolent woman stirred the potion in the pot and shouted the same incantation into the chimney: "Cowslip, cowslip! Bring in ten...." Then she singled out one, still invoking Pan Ulasovych. Then she whispered secretly: "And she who's sitting and waiting, let her be hibernating." And again, she blew on Yosypovna, and the poor thing drifted off to sleep....

For the third time the old woman continued to stir the potion, and now, with all her might, shouted through the stovepipe about the cowslip; and as she reached the final line, she let out a shrill cry from straining, shouting with all her might to summon Pan Ulasovych. Then, she blew a breath toward the cornet's daughter, saying: "And those who sleep and huff, let them snore and puff." And because of this, Panna Yosypovna dropped onto her pillows and began snoring so loudly that the whole house reverberated... And suddenly, – a thud on the house door! – followed by groaning, rumbling, and sighing... reaching from the hallway... We'll find out later what it was....

VIII

The sad and unhappy Pan Mykyta Ulasovych Zabryokha, of the illustrious town of Konotop. the captain of the valiant Konotop hundred-man company, stood there with his hands crossed, He stood on the street by the pub, where the company would always gather for drills or roll call, just in case a Kozak happened to go missing occasionally. There he stood, with his heart heavy, hands folded, head lowered, like an ox before the yoke. And all the Kozaks, the entire company, stood perfectly lined up before him. They had put their hats neatly on the tavern's bench so that when drill time came, they wouldn't fall off their heads, or that the children, who were constantly running around the Kozak camp, wouldn't fetch them and hide them somewhere. So, there the Kozaks stood, waiting to see what fate had in store for them and what orders would be given. They exchanged whispers like the sound of water gurgling in gutters, until it resounded like an echo. Some of them rummaged through their pockets for tobacco or snuff, sniffed it and sneezed, or lit and puffed their pipes right there.

Pan Zabryokha paid no mind to all this, and he neither saw nor heard what was happening around him. It seemed to him that he was still listening to what the scribe of the Konotop company, Prokip Ryhorovych Pistryak, had read to him. But that had been a while ago, and once the scribe finished reading what he needed to read, he put away the document and pocketed it. Then, Pan Ulasovych let out a deep, heavy sigh, like a blacksmith's bellows, and asked the scribe:

"Do me a favor, Ryhorovych, my friend! Please explain to me what the leport says in plain words. You know, I've never been good at understanding the written word. Even though I attended school and even started to learn the psalms, I got stuck after a couple of lines and gave up on this endeavor. So, don't read it to me, but tell me: what kind of a leport did that Kozak bring from Chernihiv? After all, we sent a leport saying we wouldn't go on campaign, even if they lash our backs a thousand times. We are too busy. We have other things to do. So why are they still bothering us?"

"The entire Chernihiv squad is enraged!" the scribe Pistryak began to say, clearing his throat, "They're drafting up mandates and scolding you, dear Captain, and me... yes, they're accusing us – pardon the expression – of being idiots, because we didn't follow their orders and didn't take a step toward Chernihiv."

"Got it, though it took me a few rounds to figure out what you were saying, Pan Scribe," Ulasovych interrupted, "So in the end, do we still have to prepare for the Chernihiv campaign?"

"Indeed, we do, no other way around it!" said Pistryak, twitching his moustache.

"May their mothers tremble in despair! Like hell we will!" He finished speaking, then started to give the fig. He kept twisting his fingers in the fig pointing toward Chernihiv and clicking his tongue. But then he shouted, "I won't go! I sent them a leport with the lame messenger saying we wouldn't go no matter what!"

To this, Pistryak replied, "Well, our lame messenger hasn't gotten even half the way there. Don't fret, dear Captain. We won't move until we receive a definitive response to our reservation."

"Precisely, precisely, Ryhorovych, we won't go! See how cleverly I've figured it? We won't go and that's that. Well, lads, the sun is setting. Disperse for dinner, and tomorrow at the crack of dawn get your scythes and set to work. Pan Scribe, let's go,have dinner at my place. Pazka has made some tasty dumplings and fried up some eggs... Oh, dear me! Oh, save me! Oh, disaster!" Suddenly, Ulasovych started shouting in a voice that wasn't his own, clutching at his sides. Pistryak and the Kozaks rushed toward him, wondering what had happened. Suddenly... rustling... he levitated and flew upward like a bird, still shouting at the top of his lungs....

Oh boy, the folks in the glorious little town of Konotop gasped in horror when they saw Pan Mykyta Zabryokha, the Captain of their brave company, take off and soar to the very heights of the heavens like a bird but with no wings needed. Women, men, kids, and even the elderly left their houses to witness this spectacle. They all tilted their heads back, gazing as Pan Zabryokha, like some exotic bird, flew beneath the heavens. His hands flapped like wings. His Circassian coat puffed up like feathers, his legs kicked as if they were possessed, his trousers were practically ready for liftoff, and he was sweating as if he'd just left the sauna. All while he flew and kept shouting. Whenever he saw a man on the ground, he would shout at the top of his lungs begging for a drink. Seeing this, the older folks spat in awe and terror; women shrieked in fright; and many a little child later had to have their fear banished with a magic spell. But was it really all that frightening?...

Upon witnessing such a wonder, Prokip Ryhorovych stood there with his head thrown back, his mouth agape like a barn door, throat visible, eyes popping out of their sockets, and he flailed his arms around trying to catch and take control of Captain Zabryokha, who had taken flight like a startled goose. And the entire Kozak fraternity, every last one of them, marveled at this comedy... And how could they not, when quite a sane man took flight like a bird? If it were midnight with all sorts of unclean spirits romping about... But the sun had just set....

Old Lyoznykha, barely emerging into the courtyard due to her age and ailments, gazed upon the Kozaks as they gathered, joked among themselves, prepared for drill exercises, and sighed, saying: "Thanks God, I'm not a Kozak! I can't even make it across my own house without getting out of breath, and they have to run around, fight, and undergo drills! I don't want to, I don't want to be a Kozak!" and she stared at them, but then... yikes! Something terrifying was flying above her. After squinting, she shuffled over to the Kozaks and began to tell them not to wait for Captain Zabryokha, because he'd already flown off into the blue yonder. "I saw it myself," she said, "he's flying like a crow, just without the 'caw,' and always begging for a drink..."

The scribe and the Kozaks could do nothing about it. They just scattered and chatted, each telling those who hadn't seen it how the Konotop Captain Mykyta Zabryokha had taken flight like a crow... And those who hadn't heard about it merely shrugged and marveled, saying: "Well, what good can we expect when even our superiors have lost their marbles?" But Prokip Ryhorovych, well, he knew what it was all about! Even though he was scared witless, he hadn't forgotten about dumplings, scrambled eggs, or Pazka, and headed over to her for dinner... and Pan Captain had already slipped his mind.

And our Pan Captain, poor thing, soared and kept soaring all the way from Konotop, not knowing where he'd end up or what fate had in store for him. And whoosh! There was a little farmstead, and he started to descend, lower and lower... He squinted and peered – yup, it was Bezverkhy Khutir, right there on Sukha Balka. Oh, he kept flying, over rooftops and into the cornet's yard, a place where he'd been many times before. Just then he flew into the yard and headed toward the cornet's house, then through the inner porch, and bumped straight into the door of the house, which was locked and bolted from the inside, thud! He fell like a battering ram! And there he stretched out like a log, not breathing, not moving a muscle....

And that's when he thudded into the house door, where Konotop's witch Yavdokha Zubykha was working her magic over the cornet's daughter.

Yavdokha promptly called out to him:

"Don't groan too loudly or moan so that no one will hear you. Get into the house quickly." She unlocked the door and called to him over and over again. But there was no response, no sign of life; our captain lay there, stiff as a board. Yavdokha had no choice but to haul him into the house herself, and just as she dragged him to another spot, he groaned, and his eyes popped open as if he had no clue where he'd ended up. Looking around, he recognized Zubykha, and he immediately began berating her parents, wondering what kind of curse she'd cast upon him. Yavdokha, meanwhile, was as sassy as ever: "Don't you know your luck when you see it? But keep your voice down, or you'll wake up all the servants. So, what can I do, huh? You got scared, really scared, it's true. But we have no time to banish your fear. Now, go ahead, give this a sniff." And she held grated horseradish under his nose. He took a whiff and sneezed three times in a row, then he started begging for a drink. Yavdokha fetched some water, whispered her spell over it, sprinkled him with that water, licked it from his forehead with her tongue making a cross sign to prevent harm to his eyes, and then let him drink the water. He downed a sizable gulp and practically emptied the jug before saying:

"Give me some more, auntie."

"Sure thing!" Zubykha said, "but I didn't summon you here to drink. Quit your whining and groaning and get to work. Look what a beauty is lying here! Pan Zabryokha glanced around with his eyes wide open, and he was taken aback to see Panna Olena sleeping on the floor... and he shivered as if he had been scalded.

Indeed, she truly looked like a queen! She was a beauty, but even more now in her deep sleep, sprawled out and blushing like your crimson jacket or a garden rose; her corset had come undone, her chemise was in disarray... and her braids, oh boy, they'd gotten so loose that they practically covered her breasts, but not entirely....

Our Ulasovych, as he beheld this regal sight, moved around the sleeping beauty like a peacock, only dancing on tiptoe, staring, drooling, and licking his lips. He forgot about his duties, all the flying he'd done, and even that he had asked for a drink. Food and water were the furthest things from his mind with such a scene unfolding before his eyes!

He was just about to devise something... Aha! That's when Yavdokha caught him by the hem of his coat, dragged him toward the oven, and said: "Get a grip on yourself, you fool! It's time to get to work, not mess around. Here, take this frog, twist its head to the side, and toss it, still alive and kicking into the hot oven." So, the Captain did exactly as Yavdokha ordered, and as that frog was croaking away, he chucked it into the oven, from which Zubykha raked out the burning wood fire onto the hearth. Once that frog was roasted and dried up, Yavdokha took it out, stripped off all the flesh, collected the bones, and began to sort through them, searching for something specific, and sure enough, she found one that was just as sharp as a skewer. She taught Ulasovych exactly what to do with it.

Pan Zabryokha pressed that sharp bone to the heart of the cornet's daughter... and suddenly, in her sleepiness, she began to talk: "What do I care about Pan Khalyavsky!... Fie on him. My sweet Mykyta, my darling! Where are you? Come to me, my sweetie. I just want to set my eyes on you..."

Ulasovych gave a loud happy laugh. If Yavdokha hadn't reined him in, he'd have launched himself at the cornet's daughter like a Kozak into battle. But Yavdokha put a stop to that with a quick tug on his arm – whoa there! – she took him aside and instructed him as to what he should do.

Next Pan Captain was by her side, pulling surprises out of his pocket. Pebbles, marbles, little trinkets – you name it – Zubykha gave it all to him. He'd grab a fistful of those treasures, hold them, give them a little shake, and slip them into another pocket. He kept it up for quite a while. Meanwhile, the cornet's daughter, half-asleep but not missing a beat, suddenly said, "Hey there, my sweet Mykyta! Ulasovych, my dear, I'm falling for you harder and harder, you know!"

Then Yavdokha handed him a curved frog's bone, and following her lead, as soon as Pan Zabryokha pricked the cornet's daughter just below the heart, she lit up and started going on, "I don't want… Khalyavsky! Don't force me to marry him. Let me marry Zabryokha. If not, I'll run away!"

So, Yavdokha pulled Ulasovych aside and said, "See, I've set it up so she will brush off Khalyavsky, and she'll be killing herself for you. Now, my friend, it's time to go home."

Ulasovych scratched his head, "Wait a minute, Auntie! Just like that, we're calling it a day?"

Zubykha raised an eyebrow, "You've had your slice of the pie, my boy. What more do you want? Now take it easy and get ready for the love letters. Let's head out."

"But how, auntie? To fly again – no way. Ugh. I can't"

"Oh lad, I am sorry for you. This time we'll not fly. Whether you doze off on the way or snooze, have no fear. We'll be back home before the sun rises. I'll be back here again tomorrow, handing Panna Olena this frog charm to keep. As long as she's got it, she's head over heels for you. So, let's set off before the young lady wakes up." And off went Zubykha, gathering her belongings, arranging them just so, clutching the tray and the spindle, and leaving the house with Ulasovych. Stepping out, she winked at Pan Zabryokha:

"Mount the tray as if you were saddling a horse, and I'll figure out where to sit. I've seen it all."

Just as Ulasovych raised his leg, Yavdokha whistled and clicked her tongue! The tray rose up, with Pan Captain sitting on top, and Yavdokha behind, giving it a whirl with her spinning wheel. She chattered away as if she were talking to a horse, and up they soared, reaching for the heavens!

So there sat our Konotop Captain, Mykyta Ulasovych Zabryokha, on that tray as if on a horse. His feet dangled without stirrups, and just to keep from falling, he gripped the edges of that tray which kept dashing faster and faster than Yatsko's stray horse. And behind Ulasovych, Zubykha was shivering from the cold wind that was howling and bothering her quite a bit.

Before they knew it, Konotop was almost in sight. Yavdokha muttered something, and suddenly the tray dipped lower and lower... and splat! It landed just by Zabryokha's gate. Ulasovych crashed on the ground and almost fainted. Thus he didn't see Yavdokha disappear with the tray and someone leave his yard through the gate. He only saw his Pazka waving goodbye to someone.

"Is that you, my dear Pan?" she asked her Ulasovych. "Where have you been so long... I've been waiting for you this whole time...."

"Why did you go out the gate?" the Captain inquired.

"What else could I do? I was so worried!" Pazka replied.

"And who was it you were seeing off from the yard?"

"Well... a stray bull had wandered in among our livestock, so I...."

"A little bull! Among the livestock! Hmm!" grumbled Captain Mykyta, heading into the house and ordering the lights to be turned on since it was dark.

Pazka brought a light into the house... Captain Zabryokha looked at the table, where there were half-eaten dumplings, two spoons, two plates, an empty pitcher, and no sign of the pear liqueur. He scowled, bit his lip, and muttered, "A bull... among the livestock!" Then he headed to the attic loft, put out the light, plopped onto his bed, thinking, "What do I care! Now I have the cornet's daughter!" and he fell into deep sleep, his snoring echoing throughout the house.

IX

The sad and unhappy Olena Yosypovna, the cornet´s daughter, having woken up, sat on her bed in her house at Bezverkhy Khutir that was on Sukha Balka. She sat there, yawned, rubbed her eyes, and couldn't quite figure out where she was, what she was, what had happened to her, what she had dreamt, and why she felt so nauseated and heavy.

And then, in walked the Konotop witch, Yavdokha Zubykha. Stepping into the house, she said:

"Good day to you, Pannochka! Why are you so sad and unhappy?"

"Oh, granny! I've remembered everything now!... What have you done to me?...," she said, sighing deeply.

"Hush now! Keep quiet and listen!" said Yavdokha. "Just put this amulet around your neck and tie this ribbon, and everything will be fine." And saying this, she put the amulet on the cornet´s daughter neck. In that amulet, there was a frog's hind leg, its dried-up heart, a piece of a frontal bone, and a bit of Mykyta's footprint. As soon as she put it on, Panna Olena brightened up, refreshed. Her eyes were sparkling, her cheeks blushed, and she couldn't sit still on the bed; she rushed toward Zubykha and even started crying and pleading:

"Auntie, dear, sweet mistress of the house! Whatever you do, just let me marry Captain Zabryokha. I am not quite sure what his first name is, but please let me marry him."

"But he courted you, and you even fed him a roasted pumpkin?"

"Oh, I was foolish and out of my mind... I didn't look at him properly, didn't ask around, didn't listen to my brother... Now my world is dark without him!"

"But don't you love Pan Khalyavsky, Omelianovych, the judge ́s son?"

"Oh, I was foolish and out of my mind! Since yesterday, I've cursed him and his pestilence upon me; I am completely over him. There's only one thing on my mind – I just want to see Captain Zabryokha, to gaze upon him, to hug him, to have him marry me." And saying this, she grabbed onto Zubykha's legs and lay down on the floor, crying and pleading: "Please, auntie, make him marry me. I'll call you my dear mother for three years, I'll respect and honor you. But if he rejects me, I'll wander the world aimlessly, bringing death upon myself...."

"All right, all right, calm down!" Yavdokha told her, raising her from the floor and seating her on a bench. "Your sweet brother will come in soon, tell him everything without embarrassment; let him ride straight to Konotop to Captain Zabryokha and tell him to send men for the embroidered towels for the wedding. And as for me, I'll go to Konotop and take care of what needs to be done with Zabryokha; don't worry, just focus on your tasks." And saying this, she left the house, while the cornet ́s daughter shouted after her: "And I'll give you a headscarf and wedding bread too...."

Just then, her little brother, the cornet ́s son, entered the house looking cheerful and rosy cheeked as if he hadn't been unwell at all. The witch's medicine had done wonders for his upset stomach.

"Hey there, my little brother, are you well?" his sister, the cornet ́s daughter, asked.

"My stomach gave me some rest only before sunrise, and I dozed off and slept like a log. But now I'm good as new," said the cornet ́s son.

"Well, sweet brother! Don't fret: soon you'll be free to join the monastery," the cornet ́s daughter started saying, her eyes cast down to the ground. "I've... chosen a fiancé for myself..." Olena said and blushed beet red from embarrassment."

"Whom?"

"Captain Zabryokha from Konotop."

"The one you treated to a roasted pumpkin?"

"Yeah!"

"But it seems like you had your eye on Pan Khalyavsky?"

"Curse him! And don't mention him. But please, do me a favor, go to Konotop and tell Pan Zabryokha to send people for the embroidered wedding cloths today, or at least tomorrow, and arrange for the wedding on Sunday."

"What is the rush about?" the cornet ́s son asked her, his stomach twisting in knots, anticipating an end to his secular life. "Maybe you could look around a bit more, instead of instead of going willy-nilly into it, as if Easter were tomorrow."

"I'd rather die than not be married to Captain Zabryokha in a week's time. I dreamt of him today: what a handsome man he is! Impeccable and rich! There's no end to his wealth: he's constantly shifting money from pocket to pocket, all sorts of coins, silver, gold, pearls, and all kinds of precious stones... Please do me a favor, dear brother, my little falcon, my little swan! Hurry as quick as you can. Bring him with you and bring people if you need to, so they can present the wedding cloths. However, we don't even need people, we can gather them here; just bring him to me, bring him to me right away!"

The malevolent Konotop witch wreaked havoc, leaving the poor girl in such a state that she was climbing the walls, wishing for Captain Ulasovych Zabryokha.

There was nothing for the cornet to do! He ordered his breakfast, ate, and pondered. Not content with that, he didn't make up his mind and wanted lunch; while having lunch, he pondered some more. After lunch, he finally made up his mind and said to himself, "Pan Khalyavsky would not even have a taste of liqueur, but holy hell, it's hard to keep up with Captain Zabryokha. Oh well! I'll let my sister marry him and live with the young couple for a year." Having deliberated thusly, he hopped on a cart and raced to Konotop, straight to Captain Mykyta Ulasovych Zabryokha.

Meanwhile, our young lady was bustling around, getting ready for the betrothal ceremony: cleaning the house, scrubbing tables and benches, rinsing dishes, plucking birds, preparing noodles, setting out pots, arranging embroidered cloths... to the point that all the hired help were overwhelmed by such early morning activity.

X

The sad and unhappy, Demyan Omelianovych Khalyavsky, the honorable judge's son, sat in his farmstead, in an empty house, from which, after getting angry, he chased everyone out. He was in a constant flux of annoyance, then melancholy, berating anyone who came to his mind, sulking the day away, consumed by sorrow to the point of overwhelming distress. And how could he not be upset? The cornet's daughter, Olena Yosypovna, from Bezverkhy Khutir on Sukha Balka, who had pledged and sworn never to marry anyone but him, who had spent many an evening with him under the willow tree by the well until midnight, exchanging rings with him, who had held him sacred in her heart, who, at the slightest hint of his return from the campaign in Chernihiv, would immediately present the embroidered wedding cloths, and relying on this, he tried very hard not to be kept in Chernihiv any longer and be allowed to marry... Escaping from Chernihiv, he rode like a madman to his own farmstead, riding day and night, exhausting his horse, and himself. All out of breath, he rushed into the house, immediately shouting for Khivrya, his maid, to call his uncles and distant cousins to him, to quickly gather holy bread and walking sticks, and ride to the cornet's daughter for the embroidered cloths... Just then, Khivrya gave him the bad tidings. "Well," she said, "the cornet's daughter is already engaged to Captain Mykyta Ulasovych Zabryokha from Konotop. They've even presented the embroidered cloths and started the matchmaking festivities, and you know what! Only those who weren't at the matchmaking weren't drunk, because everyone else lay flat out on the floor until the second rooster's crow. The wedding is tomorrow. Since the cornet's daughter is an orphan, she is wandering the streets of Konotop with her hair let down, singing songs and gathering bridesmaids. And your uncles' wives in their best garments have gone to Bezverkhy Khutir to bake a *korovai*[23] (wedding loaf). Captain Zabryokha arrived and brought a blind fiddler to play at the wedding...." As the honorable judge's son Khalyavsky listened to all this, his mouth hanging agape in astonishment, he was left dumbfounded. And then he started shivering all over, his eyes bulging out as if they were on fire, he clenched his fists, struck himself on the head, barely held himself back and felt dizzy for a while, then finally, like a coiled spring, he began to curse, berating Panna Yosypovna and her brother, Captain Zabryokha, his uncles and their wives, brothers, sisters-in-law, bridesmaids, the wedding bread-bearers, the blind fiddler, and even Khivrya... He ranted and ranted, unleashing his fury, spewing forth his disapproval, foam even gushed from his mouth as if he were rabid... Then, he lunged at Khivrya... he would have torn her to pieces had she not realized his state and fled.

Now he was left alone in the house, seething in his own thoughts, both melancholic and infuriated, pulling fistfuls of hair from his head in frustration... But when he realized that there was nothing to be done, he suddenly let out a loud, piercing cry, howling like his father's hound, and hurled himself against the wall.

For the tenth time, he was pounding his head and his chest with his fists, and just as he was about to bash his head

....

[23] For a picture of a tradition *korovai* wedding bread, which Ukrainians make instead of wedding cake, see: https://1.bp.blogspot.com/-50xbOu8txl0/XepVcwHZ_lI/AAAAAAAAL_8/fz_M3i-W3EckK5cLKCFRKoQ8glwwf_n-dACEwYBhgI/s1600/Belarus-Minsk-Bread_and_Confectionery_Business_Exhibition-8.jpg.

against the wall... rip!... an old granny, as old as the hills, entered the house, hunched over and frail, barely dragging her feet due to age, leaning on a walking stick for support.

She entered, curtsied, and said, "Good day to you, dear Pan!" But Pan remained silent, his eyes wide and breath heaving.

"Why aren't there any preparations for the big day here?" the old lady said, not caring that he was looking at her like a madman. "No birds have been plucked, no sheep have been slaughtered, and no noodles prepared! Just look at yourself! Tomorrow is your wedding, and you're dawdling – wow!"

I do not know where this old lady would have ended up or how her bones would have been crushed if Demyan Omelyanovych hadn't gotten so angry at her words, to the point where he just couldn't take it anymore! Froth filled his mouth, overflowing, and he couldn't move his tongue. He could only tremble and clench his fists, howling like a lame puppy. My guess is that if this had gone on for a bit longer, he would have burst from rage. But how could he endure it? Could there be anything worse? This is a man who had just arranged to get married and had sent people with the wedding bread, and here the girl brings him a roasted pumpkin! And which girl? The one who had been seeing him for at least a year, who had spent many a night with him under the willow tree by the well, where she swore and pledged that she would marry no one else but him; and now she marries someone else. And that someone else happens to be Captain Zabryokha from Konotop, whom she used to mock both behind his back and to his face. How could the judge's son endure that? After such a tragedy, this disgusting old woman arrives and mocks him on top of it? He felt as if he would smash her into pieces like an old pumpkin. But he was so overwhelmed that he couldn't even move, and in the meantime, she said:

"Why are you so furious? Be quiet and listen to me. I'll be damned if the cornet's daughter Olena, from Bezverkhy Khutir, isn't head over heels for you by tomorrow morning."

As soon as the old lady said this to him, he was so overwhelmed with joy that he quivered and tried to say something but couldn't. He just stared, struggling to speak, and managed to utter:

"What?"

"May I be a wicked, cursed daughter!" she exclaimed, "May my eyes pop out, my hands twist, and may I shake, may my face be covered in seven hundred spots and sores!" She began cursing with all manner of witchcraft incantations, "If I don't make sure that you and Olena are wed by tomorrow morning. Just listen to me: don't you know me well?"

Why wouldn't he know the Konotop witch, Yavdokha Zubykha (for it was indeed her)? She cured his fevers when he was a child. She had certainly made herself known to him. So, when he heard this from her, a sense of relief came over him, and he immediately knew what he had to do. He knelt before her, clasping her knees, and implored:

"Dear auntie, my cherished one! Please, do whatever it takes to make Olena mine. I will call you my dearest mother for a whole year. I'll buy you a *plakhta* (skirt), an *ochipok* (headdress), and a *serpanok* (scarf), whatever your and your cat's hearts' desire.... Just please, help me. Olena is already gathering her bridesmaids, and the wedding loaves are being baked. The Konotop Captain, Mykyta Ulasovych, has hired a blind violinist to play at the wedding, so there's no time to waste...."

"Am I not Yavdokha?" she replied. "Am I not capable of arranging or cancelling his wedding? Let him just run up costs and spend his father's money for you. I'll get him married! Let Olena gather her bridesmaids; they can start singing for Mykyta. I know they'll end up singing your name. So, get going quickly! Tell your servants to bake and cook, to sharpen whatever needs sharpening. Go gather your groomsmen, your matchmaker, your sword and candle-bearers, the elders, and find someone to be in charge of it all."

With renewed vigor, the judge's son jumped up, fastened on his belt, and reached for his hat, to get his wedding party ready. As he was about to leave, Yavdokha, stepping outside the house, began to sing a wedding song, adding a playful flourish:

"Of Demyanko's parents there are dozens,
But no close kin, not a real father.
All for drinking, and none to complain,
All for revelry, but nothing to gain.
All for merry-making and having a spree,
But none to give advice as wise as me."

XI

The sad and unhappy cornet's daughter, Olena Yosypovna, was getting dressed in her room in Bezverkhy Khutir on Sukha Balka. She was getting ready and not getting ready at the same time. She tried to hurry because the bells had already begun chiming in the village for the morning service, and now all the bells were ringing. She had to get to the church quickly, since the day before, during the matchmaking discussions, they had decided to marry her to the Konotop Captain, Pan Zabryokha, Mykyta Ulasovych. The farmstead was about five or maybe two versts away from the village. So, she had to hurry to be on time. But somehow, her hands refused to cooperate. She had already combed and braided her hair, and started to put on her ribbons, when she suddenly caught sight of her best kerchief, the one that the judge's son had given her, and she gasped for a breath. This made her remember him, and she couldn't help but shed a few tears. Zubykha saw all this and couldn't stand still. She was in and out of the room, fussing around, placing a necklace on Olena's neck, a wreath of flowers on her head, and when Olena was completely dressed, she ran out into the yard. She turned around on one foot three times counterclockwise, muttered something quietly to herself, gestured toward the village, and said:

"Whoever needed haste on this day,
Let them in their house delay,
Until the sun begins its dance,
They'll find no door nor window, by chance."

Then she went back into the house and started preparing Olena for the wedding ceremony. She instructed her to bow three times at the feet of the father and mother, who had been brought in to stand in for her deceased parents for the occasion, and then her younger brother. She gave the maid of honor a pair of five-kopeck candles for the ceremony, a handkerchief to tie the bride's hands, an embroidered cloth to stand on, and half a kopeck for a sexton to place under the cloth. Lastly, so no one could see, she quietly gave the maid of honor a tiny bone and burr, and taught her what to do with them. And so, our young bride set off for the village with her maid of honor, hurrying to the morning ceremony to marry Pan Zabryokha, the Konotop Captain, Mykyta Ulasovych.

But what was Yavdokha doing back at Bezverkhy Khutir? There was a forty-year-old maid named Solokha. Poor and destitute, she had no clothes to speak of, nothing at all. And to top it off, she was blind in one eye from a cataract; her hair had fallen out from scabies, her head was as bald as the palm of your hand; her neck was covered in hives and pimples that oozed; and she had a constant fever blister on her cheek. She was missing teeth, hunchbacked, cross-eyed, and she had a little hole instead of a nose. One leg was lame, and her right hand was so crooked she couldn't even bring it to her mouth. Having taken such a "beauty," Zubykha adorned her with ribbons, let them loose instead of braids, dressed her in borrowed finery, procured a string of beads with crosses, and placed it around her neck. Then, as she finished dressing her, Yavdokha seated her atop a walking stick. She herself sat on another and made a short clicking and kissing noise. With that, they bounded off, so fast that a cloud of dust trailed behind them. Upon reaching the village and nearing the church, Yavdokha said to Solokha, "My dear, stay in the narthex at the nave's entryway and hold this poppy flower in your hand. When a Kozak comes and takes your hand to lead you to the wedding ceremony, don't hesitate, don't procrastinate, just go and get married. Remember, you must wait until sunrise." Solokha took her position as instructed, while Yavdokha continued on her way.

As for Olena, she was on her way to the church with her maid of honor. With each step, she praised Pan Zabryokha. She extolled his virtues, his dark and handsome looks, his fine figure and agility, his Kozak moustache, and his overall attractiveness. But as they approached a crossroad, the maid of honor gently tapped Olena on the back three times with the small bone that Yavdokha had given her. "Get away, you wretch!" she whispered. "What are you, dear sister, doing, why are you pushing me from behind?" Olena asked. "Oh, dear lady, I just removed a feather that got stuck to the back of your overcoat," the maid of honor replied. Olena continued speaking about Mykyta Ulasovych, but not as fondly as before. She said he didn't have eyes as captivating as Khalyavsky, the judge's son. At the second crossroads, his moustache didn't seem to her as fine as the judge's son's either. The further they went, the less attractive he seemed to her. She found him worse and worse, more and more repulsive and repugnant. But once they reached the church, the maid of honor secretly untied the cord on which a small amulet-bag was hanging from Olena's waist. Inside the bag there was the frog's hind leg, the dried heart, and the forehead bone with the trace of Mykyta's footprint. Olena did not notice when the bag was untied, since it was so small. Suddenly, she cried out, "Damn him, curse him! I won't and don't want to marry him. Let's go back, sister." "Why go back?" the maid of honor replied. "Let's at least stay in the church for a while. If the Captain comes to wed you, just refuse right here. He'll be even more embarrassed if you make a scene in public." "That's true," Olena said. "I'll tell him off right here. Let's go into the church."

So, she entered the church. Panna Yosypovna looked around, but there was no Pan Ulasovych. The morning service was in full swing. She turned as red as a poppy and then as white as linen. Her heart raced; she feared lest he should come in and drag her into marriage. Just as they finished reading up to "and the next day that we were," the door creaked open: bridesmaids, sword and candle-bearers, matchmakers, the best man, the groomsman, elders; they were all far from simple folks, all from the gentry, wearing tunics, Circassian coats, and such fancy dresses that you'd drool! Their garments looked even fancier than those of our village deacon who once studied philosophy and, after marrying our deaconess, became the village priest. And behind this wedding procession walked a young man... Who could that be? Olena trembled as if she had been struck by lightning when she realized it wasn't Pan Ulasovych, the Konotop Captain, but instead Pan Judge's son Khalyavsky, whom she loved so dearly. And then, the maid of honor subtly pushed her with the little burr that the witch had given her and whispered softly, "Stick to him again." After this, Olena blushed so much that she squeezed through the crowd and made her way to Pan Khalyavsky. She grabbed his hand and said, "Take me! Take me as your wife no matter what! If you have another woman, show me where she is, I swear I'll scratch her eyes out right here. I was infatuated before, and now I'll die if you abandon me...." "But that's why, my lady, I came, to marry you," said Pan Judge's son and pulled her by the hand toward the altar where the priest was waiting. Without delay, they sang the "Fruitful Vine," performed the ritual where they walked around the altar three times and asked the bridegroom to kiss the bride. They charged the groom a half-kopek coin for the service, and sent them home in peace, while some stayed in church to put out the candles and such.

XII

The sad and unhappy Pan Konotop Captain Mykyta Ulasovych Zabryokha, paced around in his house, dressed as handsomely as he could, groomed himself immaculately, and neatly trimmed his scalp lock. He paced about the house where he had arrived from Konotop the evening before, all to be wedded to the cornet's daughter Yosypovna this morning, as they had arranged just the day before. The church bells had just chimed for the morning service, and he sprang up, waking up the scribe Pan Pistryak, Ryhorovych, whom he had summoned to be his best man.

While the bells were ringing, our Kozaks were shaving and getting dressed. And when it was time, they put on their new boots and finery and started making their way out.

"Come on, Pan Ulasovych, just open that door. Time waits for no one. Come on, come on! What's with the hesitation at the latch? Break it open; open the door," commanded Pan Ryhorovych to Pan Captain, who was fumbling at the door with no success.

"Indeed!" said Mykyta Ulasovych, "You open it if you can find it. Look, there is no door!"

"Why on earth are you jesting with me?" the scribe exclaimed. "The door is there, just pull the latch...."

"What latch are you talking about? There's a bare wall here, no door to be seen! Look for yourself!"

Pan Pistryak threw himself at it... grab, grab! Tug, tug! But there was no door, and the latch was nowhere to be found; the wall itself seemed to have closed in on him. He searched, and searched – until he got tired, cursed at the wall, and his companion took over, feeling all around – still, there was no door to be found!

"What kind of dark sorcery is this? Where has the door gone?" Pan Zabryokha grumbled and clenched his teeth, gnashing them in frustration because the bells had been ringing for quite some time now.

"I saw the door opening, here and there, and now it's gone!" Ryhorovych roared, his temper flaring until he almost tore his hair out. Then he said, "What shall we do, Pan Captain? Let's extend our arms and examine until we perceive some point of junction, and we shall keep doing this until we locate the seam."

"Tell me plainly, Pan Scribe! Forget this Holy Writ speaking," he was saying "I can't comprehend this as it is, and you are still trying to dig into it with your Holy Writ talk. Speak plainly!" Pan Ulasovych pleaded; his eyes filled with tears. "Just say it simply."

"Spreading arms, feeling, a connection point – in simple terms, groping. Place your right hand in my left palm, and we'll grope together, circling the entire house, until we find where the door should be or whether there's an enemy with malicious intent trying to hide it."

With great effort, Pan Mykyta finally figured out what the scribe proposed. So, they began to grope along the wall. One went one direction, the other went the opposite: pat, pat! grab, grab! "Found anything, Ryhorovych?" "Nothing! It vanished like smoke." "Let's keep going." They continued. "Have you found anything, Pan Ulasovych?" "Phew! I wish they'd burn in hell! And the bells are ringing vigorously. Oh, what a headache!"

They felt all over the house, came together... still no door. They split again, one groping clockwise, the other counterclockwise... They reunited... nothing! They'd be happy to find even a small window, but that had vanished too. Both started crying. Pan Mykyta Ulasovych sat down on the floor and began lamenting aloud, "Morning service is over, and Panna Cornet's Daughter must have waited and waited and might have gone home. Oh, dear!" Meanwhile, Pan Pistryak seemed to have come up with something of his own. He stood in the middle of the room, gestured with his fingers, and just as he was about to say something... a clinking sound! The latch! The door opened! In walked Yavdokha Zubykha, their friend, the Konotop witch, who had cast this spell on them and hidden the door. She scolded them:

"Have you gone mad or just lost your minds? What business do you have here? Why aren't you going to get married? However, the people attending the morning service will have left the church. The bride and her bridesmaids have been waiting for a long time, and here you are wasting time."

"Oh, auntie!" Pan Zabryokha barely managed to utter. "It's a disaster here."

"Confusion has occurred," said Ryhorovych, squinting at Zubykha. "This door, which hath been produced by means of all of mankind, was lost. And it hast returned, but how pray tell? I know not!"

"Tell me in plain terms, Pan Mykyta, because no one can understand what he has just said. What kind of ghostly apparition was going on here?" asked Yavdokha, pretending she knew nothing.

"Well, you see," said Pan Zabryokha, "it's a bit complicated to explain. Someone had stolen our door! We were groping for it, feeling all around for it, and we had to shout for help, and that's when you came in."

"Oh, oh, oh! I know, I know!" the witch exclaimed. "See, my dear boy, what mischief she has done here? I'll get even with her no doubt. She wants to play an even bigger trick on you, but don't be upset. Just go with your best man quickly to the church and take your bride. Don't scrutinize whether she's Olena or not, just take the one standing in the narthex at the nave's entryway, holding a poppy flower. Don't be too picky, and even if you see Olena somewhere, don't rush; it won't be her, the one with the poppy is yours. Look, the wife of Khalyavsky's uncle has come from Kyiv. She's more wicked than me, but she doesn't know as much as I do. She stole your door first, and now she's sent this curse on Olena, as if she's blind, lame, and pockmarked, as if she's not Olena at all. So, don't waste time, so that bitch doesn't mock us. Go ahead and get married, and when you return from the ceremony, I'll undo all this mess, and I'll drive that old hag away. Go now, quickly."

As she spoke, she glanced at Ryhorovych and winked at him, and he chuckled to himself and thought, "I figured it out!"

Thus, thanking Yavdokha for everything, our lads went off in a hurry. By the time they reached the church, everyone had already left, leaving only the priests tidying up and some people changing candles and such. There was no sign of Pan Khalyavsky with his bride, or their wedding procession. Solokha stood in the narthex at the entryway to the nave holding a poppy in her hand and waiting for her groom. Pan Mykyta stared at her, and he felt a chill in his spine. What a beauty, indeed. He looked at her with a heavy heart and said:

"What kind of a hideous apparition is this?"

"I think," said the scribe, "that she's one of King Herod's seventy daughters, whom he, the wretched one, brought forth to destroy the Christian race. One is a fever, the other a pyrexia, the third an ague, the fourth a rash, the fifth a plague, and so on, beyond counting. As for me...."

"Stop thinking just answer my question. Is she a werewolf or is she really like that?"

"Oh, my lord. When I look at her with my rational eyes, I see Panna Olena, the cornet's daughter, a magnificent maiden. However, when I examine her with my sinful, fleshly eyes, I find her covered in sores worse than all the abominations on the face of the earth. I think this is the enchantment of the highly intelligent Yavdokha, or rather, Zubykha, who arranged this to mock the threefold-anathematic accursed witch from Kyiv."

"So, Pan Scribe, shall I marry her?" inquired Pan Zabryokha.

"Well, marry her, my good sir. If your conscience doesn't object, marry her. After the consummation, all enchantment will disappear like smoke and scatter like dust in the wind," replied the scribe.

Pan Ulasovych Zabryokha straightened his stomach and approached Solokha, saying,

"Will you, my lady, marry me?"

Solokha croaked back, "I will."

They immediately took each other by the hands, like doves, entered the church and headed to the altar. Without delay, the wedding ritual was performed, and the priest said, "Now, kiss each other!" Pan Zabryokha, without looking too closely, wiped his mustaches and kissed his beautiful bride passionately, so that the entire church could hear. He even threw five altyns to the priests and left with his young bride for Bezverkhy Khutir.

The best man, Pan Pistryak, was rolling on the ground with laughter, running around the village, gathering his party to quickly take a seat at the wedding table.

XIII

The sad and unhappy Konotop Captain Mykyta Ulasovych Zabryokha stood near the manor houses in Bezverkhy Khutir. His head bowed down to his chest as he watched Panna Olena Yosypovna, the cornet's daughter, sit at the head of the wedding table with Demyan Omelyanovych Khalyavsky, the judge's son. And standing beside him was... Solokha! A beautiful maiden, neat and well-dressed in borrowed attire. Whether a *plakhta* (skirt), a *svyta* (overcoat), a necklace, or ribbons, everything that had been lent for the wedding was taken back by people, and she remained bald and barefoot, in a simple shirt, ragged and torn, wrapped in an old skirt. That's all she wore! It was Yavdokha Zubykha, the Konotop witch, who had arranged this mischief for him due to the commotion he had caused her at the river. But it wasn't even him. It was Pan Pistryak who had got even with her but had planted the idea into Pan Captain's head, and well, you know how things go in this world. If a scribe idles, he gets away with it; if a judge, unaware of the matter, signs it, he's responsible; all the bad falls on him.

Pan Ulasovych stood there for a long while, scratching his head, not knowing what to do anymore in this world. He wished he could run to the ends of the earth, but he couldn't break the marriage vow he took. He had declared in church that he "would not leave her until death separates them." But when he glanced out the window, he saw his Panna Olena sitting next to Pan Khalyavsky. And when he listened closely to the wedding songs in which the bridesmaids changed his name for the judge's son's; when he heard the "Derbensky March" played by the blind fiddler in the hallway; when he saw the witch Yavdokha Zubykha sitting in the mother's seat in red leather boots with spurs on her heels, wearing a head-dress gifted by the son-in-law, Pan Khalyavsky; when he saw her peering out the window and mocking him– he couldn't help pounding his fists and clenching his teeth.

Pan Ryhorovych was about to abandon his duties as best man and join the other wedding. He could see that there was plenty of food, plenty of *horilka*, and everyone was downing one shot after another indiscriminately. Some had already had their fifth drink. But when he tried to grab one, they wouldn't even let him in, saying, "Go to your own wedding." So, he thought to himself, "I'll leave the living behind and go bury the dead." The scribe spat over the threshold and went to his own estate.

He gathered his people and said, "Well, Pan Captain, whatever beer you've brewed, that's what we'll drink. Why waste time staring here? We need to attend to our own busi-ness. Let's go to Konotop, we'll finish what we started accord-ing to the law; the sun is high already."

They rode toward Konotop, arrived, set things more or less in order, found some belongings from Pan Ulasovych's mother, and covered Solokha's sinful body. She looked a bit less repulsive this way. They seated the newlyweds at the ta-ble, and there were all kinds of food, *horilka*, and even honey vodka. It had to be said, they were thorough about it.

Whether the bridesmaids sang or not, whether the young men danced with the girls or not, they quickly divid-ed the wedding bread and put the young couple to bed. Pan Ulasovych sighed heavily, remembering the soft pillows he would have slept on with the cornet's daughter, and all the other things. But here he had to lie down on his own bed-ding, and with Solokha, who had a pockmarked face. And to make matters worse, when he was preparing to marry Panna

Yosypovna, he had let his maid Pazka, who would always run her fingers through his hair after lunch, go to work for the scribe for the same reason. And sitting on the wedding throne with Solokha, when he saw Pazka, who had come to the wedding to watch, his teeth were set on edge....

Well, they spent the night together somehow. Despite Solokha's looks, the one who performed the role of the mother had to upbraid her hair as required by tradition.[24]

In the morning, Pan Ulasovych felt even worse when he saw Pan Khalyavsky and his young wife happily rushing to get covered. Ahead of them on a long stick they carried their silk wedding sheet marked with *kalyna* – an eloquent proof of the bride's prenuptial virginity as crimson as a guelder rose. Crimson ribbons were tied to the horses' manes and to the violinist's arms, scalp lock and mustache as well as to the violin itself. The newlyweds received their blessing in the church and had their heads covered. Everything was splendid. Pan Ulasovych, on the other hand, had nothing of the sort. His wife had both a headband and a scarf, but no *kalyna*. It was unfortunate for our Pan Zabryokha, and that's that!

People gathered, prepared to divide the wedding bread, and discussed what gifts to give Pan Zabryokha. "He's far from the best, but after all he is the captain and in charge of a hundred-man company, a leader. You can't just give him some yarn. He'll pay us back someday." So, they discussed among themselves. One wanted to give him a lamb, another a piglet, another a calf. And Pan Pistryak, as the scribe, took charcoal in hand and was about to write down on the wall what each person would give as a gift. And the groomsman was going to shout what kind of livestock each person would give... when suddenly a Kozak from Chernihiv ran in and

....

[24] For a discussion of the elements of the traditional Ukrainian wedding, see: https://www.encyclopediaofukraine.com/display.asp?linkpath=pages%5CW%5CE%5CWedding.htm.

handed a letter to Pan Captain from the colonel of Chernihiv himself.

Our Pan Zabryokha puffed up like a turkey and began to shout, urging everyone to hush, and he said, "Quiet down, everyone! Pan Scribe, go ahead and read this leport. I am busy now sitting on the wedding throne. I am a groom. But read it, read it! Is there any news or a favor in it? And read it louder!"

While Pan Pistryak slowly read the headings, there was nothing unusual. But when he went on reading, oh my!... oh my!... that's all he said. The letter stated that Pan Ulasovych Zabryokha had failed to heed the Colonel's orders and did not arrive in Chernihiv with his gallant Konotop company, as he had been instructed. Instead, he had indulged in dousing Konotop's young women and old grannies in a pond, drowning half a dozen of them. Furthermore, after spotting a witch among the ladies, he had been seen consorting with her, submitting to her, and even pledging his soul to the devil. He then soared into the sky like an exotic bird, visible to everyone, bewildering and terrifying many, even causing some small children to be so frightened that their fears had to be removed with a spell. That's how well the captain managed his company for which he was now dismissed from his post.

Upon hearing this news, the people were horrified, standing there with their mouths agape. Our dear Zabryokha sat there unable to speak as if he had choked on hot borscht. He wanted to say something, but words got stuck in his throat. He turned pale, then ashen, stopped in his tracks, and shed tears. And Pan Ryhorovych said to him, "That's how it is, Pan Cap... or now just Pan Mykyta! This is what you deserve. You already showed you had a sharp mind, ignoring the scribe's advice, flying off to heaven and blowing your company. So now we've read the first page, and let's turn to the second to see what it says. Maybe luck is on our side. All of you, keep quiet and listen; whoever I announce to be the new captain, bow to him and go to bring gifts to him."

Then he flipped over the paper, smoothed out his mustache, looked at everyone to ensure they were paying attention, and cleared his throat three times, as a schoolteacher would. Then he began to read. When he found out that he was not appointed as the Konotop company captain—as he had hoped and genuinely believed and for which he had set up Pan Zabryokha who was

replaced with another captain from a different company, Demyan Omelyanovych, Pan Khalyavsky – he dropped the letter and he lowered his head, deep in thought. Eventually, he raised his head and said to himself, "For naught! I'll butter up the new captain and will end up getting what I want. His term won't last long. I'll plot his downfall. I'll make a fool of him, and they'll replace him. Then I'll surely be in charge. Stay here, Pan Captain, or whatever you are, with your Solokha, and I'll go to the new company captain, Demyan Omelyanovych. I'll bring him the gift that I prepared for your wedding. Who's coming with me, lads?"

"I am! I am! I am!" The crowd roared, rushing out of the house, ignoring that the glasses were still full, and the wedding bread had been sliced. And that's how it was: everyone, the best man, the groomsman, the matchmakers – everyone dispersed. Only Mykyta and Solokha remained, and there was no one to eat the food that had been prepared for the feast.

So ended the wedding of Mykyta Ulasovych Zabryokha, who was once the captain of the famous military company in the town of Konotop.

XIV

The sad and unhappy Konotop scribe Prokip Ryhorovych Pistryak entered Pan Mykyta Ulasovych Zabryokha's house on the second day. Upon entering, he shuffled over to the bench, leaned on the table, and sighed.

"Don't add to my troubles, Ryhorovych," Mykyta said to him. "Things are already miserable enough in this world. Why are you howling like a dog? Has the itch gotten to your Pazka, just like it did to my Solokha?"

"May all the world's Solokhas, Pazkas, and Yavdokhas get the itch; I couldn't care less. Woe, Mykyta, woe has befallen my insides to the point of irritation!"

"What concern is that to me?" Mykyta replied, remembering how Pistryak had distanced himself after hearing he'd been replaced, offering no advice and even mocking him to his face.

"Forget about my past misdeeds, my friend! I, too, have been a sinner wandering in the wide world."

Mykyta Ulasovych asked, "Is that so?" and Pistryak, in his own unique, writerly manner, explained how he had gone to the new captain of the brave Konotop company, Pan Demyan Omelianovych Khalyavsky. He described how the new captain had looked at him arrogantly and with an unclean heart, like one would look at a stinking dog. He was ordered to write a report to the esteemed Colonel about this and that matter. Eager to outsmart the new captain, to make him play to his tune and not have him become too harsh with him, Pistryak wrote it in his own manner. But the captain was literate and quickly figured out what was wrong and said "This is wrong," and Pistryak replied, "No, it isn't. I am the scribe, and I know how and what to write." When the captain became angrier and yelled, "Write it my way!" Pistryak retorted, "I am a scribe, and I know what I'm doing!" Then the captain lost his temper and shouted, "So you're not a scribe anymore, you scoundrel!" He began to berate Zabryokha's parents and then Pistryak's, criticizing him from every angle. Finally, the captain drove him out of the house, replaced him in his position, and appointed a new scribe, a semiliterate green-beaked joker. "As a result," Pistryak concluded, "I hath been scolded and b'rat'd m're times than I can counteth."

Mykyta Ulasovych asked Pistryak, "Please tell me, Ryhorovych who could have devised such a wicked scheme for us?"

"Alas, my friend," Pistryak sighed, "the enemy of all mankind, Yavdokha Zubykha, the renowned witch of the illustrious town of Konotop, is responsible for that. She took revenge on you and made you fly like a bird. She ensnared even the honorable cornet's daughter, now Pani Khalyavska. And that's not all – oh no! She disrupted your life by arranging your marriage. She mocked us by stealing the door; she replaced the lovely Pani Olena with, God forgive me, this monstrous figure of Solokha, may she live long and prosper, and married you to her. She is the source of all this. She orchestrated all these misfortunes as revenge for our mockery of her and our attempts to thwart her. Therefore, instead of a mere thrashing we should have burnt her at the stake like a pagan, a charlatan, a heretic, like a real foe.

"We should file a leport against her," said Zabryokha. "Let her pay for the dishonor she's brought upon us by dismissing us and marrying me off to Solokha. They should throw her into the stocks...."

"Whoa!" sighed Pistryak. "No one hast power over her now. The Captain's wife gave her all sorts of luxurious headscarves, and a new *plakhta* (skirt). Captain Khalyavsky assigned an indentured servant to her and gave her a horse, a messenger, and a servant to cut wood, fetch water, and feed the cat. She was granted authority over the entire land to bewitch, enchant, and mock for the rest of her life."

"So, do you know what we'll do? We'll invite her as if we're on good terms, offer her food and drink, and then play tricks on her. We'll teach her a lesson and knock out the last few teeth she has."

"Forget about her, my friend. Better yet order that a pitcher be brought in with something good. We should drink away our sorrow, and we will both feel much better."

"Yes, let's drink then!"

And so, Ulasovych called Solokha, who brought in and poured what they needed. They began to drink. Upon downing quite a few pitchers in sorrow, they barely made their way back to their quarters. After that they would get together every day to commiserate and chat, because there was nothing more for them to do. Their best days in power were over!

EPILOGUE

This story, or fairytale, was told to me by the late Panas Mesyura, if you know who he was. It's quite lengthy. In it, Pan Khalyavsky, Demyan Omelianovych, after replacing Pan Zabryokha, Mykyta Ulasovych, was swiftly removed from the captain's position in the illustrious town of Konotop for displeasing the authorities. His wife, Olena Yosypovna, the cornet's daughter who used to live in Bezverkhy Khutir, on Sukha Balka, somehow... I'm not sure what happened or how, but for some offence she committed, her husband knocked off her headwear, tore off all her braids, and blackened her eyes. Then, he dragged her like that through the streets of Konotop after which, the young lad who had become the new scribe in place of Prokip Ryhorovych Pistryak, a handsome, dark-haired fellow, had half his head shaved and was chased away....

All these misfortunes befell them for the following reasons:

On Pan Zabryokha for his reliance on the scribe. He should have acted on his own and acted justly, like a true leader. He should have listened to the orders from above. Instead of doing what the superiors commanded, perhaps even to defend his land from the enemy, he set out to exorcise women. Presumably, drowning witches would bring rain to the land. It was as if the witches had the power to counteract the will of the heavens. Everything unfolds according to God's will. Thus, he would not do any harm to people anymore by trying to drown witches, since it was clear how many lives he had needlessly claimed in the process. Thus, he would avoid becoming involved in witchcraft and leaving benevolent God behind. Through his servant Zubykha, the devil had his way with Zabryokha so that he could fly like a goose, to the amusement of the people!

On Ryhorovych Pistryak – so that he would not deceive his chief, twist things wrongly, but instead, do his job faithfully and tell the captain the entire truth. So that, when angry with people, he would not bring harm to them like he did to the women: he ruined so many souls, whoever made him angry; he drowned them in water and left orphans. And, most importantly, he should not have drunk *horilka* to excess.

As for Pan Khalyavsky and his wife, things did not go smoothly for them either. Why did they rush to the witch? Why did they marry through spells and charms, abandoning the holy law? Ah! Although they entered into matrimony, it was not through God's will, but through Yavdokha's, and her burr and dried frog's bones. So, everything fell apart.

And as for Zubykha, you would wish her fate to your worst foe! While Pan Khalyavsky was the Konotop captain, she lived in luxury. She had a servant, and a maid appointed by the captain as her serving girl, and people used to come to her with gifts right after visiting the captain's wife. No one dared to call her a witch or even anything derogatory. They addressed her politely as Semenovna or Pani Zubykha. That's how far things had gone! But when Pan Khalyavsky was replaced, the whole world spat on her. She fell ill quickly, wasted away, and soon died. But not immediately. What she suffered! She was dying but not dying, and she couldn't move her hands or feet, but she groaned so loudly that you could hear it from the street. And her cat wandered around and mewed at the top of his lungs. What a horror! Then they tore down the ceiling, and an entirely black raven appeared out of nowhere. Flying into the house, it circled above her, flapped its wings, and then, Amen... she died with a grin on her face!

And the cat burst like a bubble. As for the raven, who knows where it flew! Burying her like a Christian was out of the question. They dragged her out of the village, buried her in a pit, nailed her with an aspen stake, and put planks over it so that she couldn't jump out. A dog dies a dog's death!

So, that's the Konotop witch for you!

TUMBLEWEED

Dedicated to Evhen Pavlovych Hrebinka[25]

---

[25] (1812-1848). Ukrainian Romantic writer who was born in the
province of Poltava and later moved to St. Petersburg in Russia where
he taught in military schools and the Institute of Mining Engineers.
Like Kvitka-Osnovyanenko, he wrote in Ukrainian and Russian. He
was quite active in St. Petersburg literary circles. He was instrumental
in helping to arrange for the release of the great Ukrainian bard Taras
Shevchenko from serfdom and in publishing the latter's pathbreaking
collection of poetry *Kobzar* (The Kobza Player) in 1840.

Do you know, good people, that this is God's judgment? A man out of anger will do harm to another, steal something, beat him, kill him altogether, but if no one sees what he has done, if no one has evidence against him, if witnesses can t prove it, that man does not care and fears nothing, and thinks that he will get away with it. Even if he is put on trial, if there is no proof or there are no witnesses, he hopes that he will elude punishment, and that he will be in the right, as if he had done nothing wrong. Oh, no! This is not true, for our Creator is above us. He, being the holiest of holies, is the truest good, the purest truth. He will not let any evil deed go unpunished. Though a man has done evil and has hidden the evidence in such a way that no other man will find the truth, He, the highest of wisdom, He, who knows our deeds and sees our very thoughts, He will not tolerate any unrighteousness. He will make known your deeds through what you might not fathom, and as though with his hand he will point it out: this is the one who has wronged his brother and turned away the accusation from himself, so that they will think of anyone else but him, so that he himself may stand pure and righteous before men. And if others even slightly forget about this matter, that man will commit an act even worse. Such a thing certainly will be revealed, and on an unexpected occasion, and because of such lack of action, you will not hope at all. But when these things are revealed, all evil deeds will also be revealed, about which people have already forgotten to investigate, because the evidence had been well hidden. Here everything will appear, everything will be revealed, by a thread, as they say, that will amass into the size of a ball. For at first, God, as a father to His children, has kept waiting, endured everything for a long time, hoping that perhaps they might come to their senses; perhaps they will stop doing wicked things, they will pray for their sins; and then they will receive forgiveness. But if not, not only do they not stop doing evil, not only do they not repent for their previous sins, but what happens further, it all ends up being worse, it goes from bad to worse. Then when it is too much, He will command forth... And an insect will be a witness, and the thread will begin to speak, and through it colossal, vile deeds will be revealed.

In one village, chickens began to vanish. Overnight, a chicken will disappear in one yard, in a second yard three, sometimes more. The housewives are worried, complaining to their menfolk, and they are indifferent: a chicken is a small matter. Maybe it ran off somewhere and was crushed by something. Further and further the chickens disappeared more and more, but the household could no longer tolerate it, so they went over to the municipality.

"Against whom you have an allegation, say so. I will not even spare my own brother, if only there should be truth to prove it," that is what the village head said.

People began to look out for any trail happening to lead to someone. What then? A chicken was taken, carried off. It was plucked on the way, and the feathers fell in Yavtushyn's yard. There were two boys there, and they were mischievous, and it had been more than a week since they had been at home. They had gone off with their father in a lorry.

"An allegation!" The head said. "One steals and turns misfortune toward someone else."

There, the trail led all the way to Kakhybida's house. What now? There are no boys there. There is only one old man, who is old and weak. He did not have the strength to go after chickens. And there are young women and girls in the family. Why would they need chickens? They have their own, good heavens! So, all is lost, and the trail is lost. Who will get to the truth? There was a young ox missing, and in a while, around a certain time, a pair of good oxen were gone. So, what was this? They were just taken from the yard, as though they had vanished into thin air. The people are sad and keep wondering. No trace of them, not a clue. No matter where the farmstead owner goes, wherever he asks questions, nothing comes of it, as though all has vanished into thin air. The people are sad and keep wondering, "What kind of wicked mother did this?" That's how they reasoned with each other. "If, say, we were quartering soldiers, it would be this way: you cannot protect yourself from a Russky soldier. On the other hand, you cannot hear a single Russky soldier for fifty miles, and no one comes to our village. It's all our own people here, and there is a thief among us! Whose honor to question, whom to think of? All of the young guys as one. We know them all, all of them are honest, all are good, all are peaceful, not a single one of them larks about, but each one of them regrets that we have this problem, and each one of them boasts that if anyone is caught, no mercy will be shown on such and such a person. It was getting dark but they couldn t call it a day, since they didn t have any clue or any suspect. We have already asked fortune-tellers, as they say, in passing: a red-haired man, they say, a Russky soldier. First, they say, he will cast a deep sleep over the entire village and then sneak around as though he were in his own house. So, what can you do against an evil word? Only have regrets from such misfortune and then be silent."

And they remained silent, but only heard that Myrin had lost everything. The last of the oxen had been led out; and there Ulas was deprived of his nag, and Marko had three wild boars taken from his pigpen, and they were already well-fed for slaughter. There was misfortune all around. Things had been lost from everywhere!

And then they heard that the entire pantry s stock has been taken away from Demyan Ridkoplyui. You dug in, you son of the enemy! What is more? He took everything, everything, both the women's and girls' stuff, and everything that was earned with hard labor was taken away, and there was not a trace of it, as if it had disappeared.

The people were wondering, and as they walked by the municipal building, they slapped their coat flaps, and everyone expected such misfortune for himself that evening. The village head dropped by and said that he didn't know what to do!

"Catch the thief for me," he said, "who is stealing from us! I'll... I'll get... He will rot in a cold prison cell!"

"We would be happy to catch him if we knew who he was," the people replied in sadness.

And then one young man, Denys Lyskotun, made himself be heard and said:

"Allow us to search all the yards! It is already obvious that no strangers have done this, it surely must be our own people."

"Why not? What he said makes sense," the old men reasoned. "Order, Pan Village Head, the most agile of lads to search the houses everywhere."

"There is no one to send," said the village head, "let Denys go, taking some boys with him."

"Maybe you won't believe me," Denys asked, elusive as he usually was.

"If we can't believe you, who can we believe?" The old men responded.

And how can you not believe Denys? What a brave lad he was, despite being an orphan without a father! He had just grown up a little and barely reached his teenage years, and it was already clear that he would become a real man. He didn't stay at home much. He didn't really like peasant labor like everyone else. He went to the villages, who knew where, to earn money. He earned so much that he soon returned, and what he did not bring home with him! He dressed just like a city-dweller, and all his clothes were fine, and his pockets filled with money. To his mother, who was already old, he would also bring a kerchief, a *plakhotka*[26], a belt, boots, and sometimes a *serpanok*[27], and he showed respect to her in every way. And he was handsome and agile. As opposed to everyone else he was different, a witty jokester and a prankster. At evening parties, you could hear only him. He was not afraid of anyone or anything. In the dead of midnight, if you told him to go to the cemetery, he would go and do everything as if it were during the day. He was only afraid of dogs. He really hated them! If there happened to be a really nasty dog in the village, he would pay any price for it, then he would hang it on a branch and beat it to death. "Well," he says, "I can t help it. I really hate dogs. I'm repulsed by them. I get all aquiver when I see them and need to kill them! I can t help it." And his cleverness knew no equal. He did not follow the life of the community closely nor did he often participate in it, but when he did go out to the municipal building and listened to what was being discussed, he would toss out a word, such that even ten gray-haired old men would not be able to come up with anything like that in three years. Everybody, everybody in the village said in unison: "Here is our new village head growing up before us!"

How could you not trust one like him to look around the yards to see if anyone has stolen things? And how! Here they began to beg him to do them a favor, to gather several young men to go inspect all the yards without overlooking a single one of them.

There was nothing else for Denys to do. He chose the young guys and set off with them.

"Start in my yard," Denys ordered.

....

[26] A long wraparound skirt.

[27] A married woman's wraparound headdress.

"But how can anyone think you did it?" The lads said. "You would be the last person suspected!"

"Well, brothers, let's do it! If we are charged with searching everybody, what kind of big shot am I not to be searched! Search, search! Maybe you'll find something," Denys said, smiling, and, holding his sides, put on his Kozak hat acock and spit through his lip the way a Russky soldier would.

"Well, what can we find!" The guys said and followed Denys. He led them into the house, into the pantry, into the attic, and wherever there was a nook. He showed them everything, to everyone, and he opened the chests, and he rummaged through everything in them. "Look," he said, "look thoroughly!"

What then? They rummaged through, sorted out everything, and if there was nothing, there was nothing. After that, they went to another yard.

There was something amiss. Here everyone more brazenly searched both the house and the yard. And Denys, taking no one with him, clambered into the attic, and what was there? He rummaged everything that he found, whether it was flax, or spinning yarn, or some roots, he went through all of it and looked in the eaves, so that at least he could find a thread of the stolen things.

Oh, but not everywhere and like that! In one yard, in the attic, in the house, Denys found a good belt made of flaxen cloth and showed it to the owner who had walked there with him. "And so it is, Kozak, this is mine, my father's belt. I gave it to my son to wear, and he put it in his mother's chest. That's right! Everything has been taken from the chest; be so kind to search to see if you can find anything else."

At this point, Denys sent the young men to the house to do a search, had the hands of both the old and the young bound, and then sent them to the municipal building. Finding nothing else there, they went to the next yard. After going to several yards, they again found a kerchief, a cap, or something similar. Denys searched everything in the eaves. Perhaps he searched more carefully than anyone else, but no one other than he found anything. Where they did find something, they took all the members of the household to the municipal building so that the entire dungeon became filled with men, women, girls, and small children.

They began to interrogate them and to write reports about each one. Each one of the families replied in the same say: "We don't know nuthin'! Everyone saw that I was not at home. I would never ever commit such a vile deed!" Everyone said the same thing. No one confessed to anything, and there was no evidence. "So, what if you found someone's belt in the attic, or a plakhta? Maybe some idler was puttering around, stole from the pantry, and scattered things in other yards so that no one would suspect him!" Denys Lyskotun remarked, pulling out a pipe from behind his bootleg... And what a wonderful thing it was! It was made from the root of a tree with a tiny lid and a little copper chain. "See to it that no one is accused to no purpose."

"It's true, it's true," the head of the village said, who, grabbing his gray beard in his hand, sat silently, and thought about what he should do here. "True," he said, "release the people from the dungeon. They are innocent. Perhaps, indeed, things were planted on them. What a smart-ass this Denys was! I realized it right now. After all, I tried to figure it out myself and consulted with elders. No one else had ever thought of it. It's true that our new village head is growing up, may he be healthy!

Denys traipsed around the village for about two days, reigned on the street, gave more than one girl a push lovingly, tore off the sleeve of more than one of them to keep her from running away from him. He taught more than ten young men to sing Russky songs, which he himself had learned by going around everywhere. He pried apart several couples about to get into an altercation. He gave numerous pieces of advice to the village head on what to do with those not paying their social duties, or to the ataman, arranging for lorries for the roads. He helped more than one homeowner to make fencing and advised on how many stacks of grain should be thrashed with a flail. Our Denys was a master of all trades. Having worked and walked around like this, he again set off from his village to work for several weeks. And all the householders and the girls missed him beyond measure!

"Is it just a bad luck, Trokhym, or what!" thus the old widow Vengerykha said to her son, who went to work in the city for two weeks, but he ended up just eating there and bringing nothing home. So, his mother, upset, said to him: "Everybody, everybody earns much money, and everybody takes care of their household and becomes rich, but you can't get anything so you can start living like other people. The little bit that I had after your father died, I've spent on your wedding. I thought we would earn money later and my daughter-in-law would help. My daughter-in-law works night and day, but I came down with something serious. Instead of waiting for help from me, you need to work to help me. Then the children were born. The boy is already six years old. He took ill. He needs to be supported. Then there are the two girls. They can't work yet, but they beg for food. They need to be fed. It's always give, give, give. And you, son, have only your hands – you won't be able to give enough. So, I say, maybe, you have had bad luck. People travel for work or even make money here. They are always earning money. They are building up their wealth. And you, even if you stay here, or go somewhere, whatever you make is just for our daily bread; to say nothing about buying something for the household. If you were able to get at least some kind of nag, then everything would be better, you could start a second job, and there could be more income.

"What can I do, mother?" Trokhym asked. "I can see for myself that there is no luck in anything I do. I work, Mom, till I sweat blood and I can't do it anymore. The employers, upon seeing that I am so listless and gaunt, are not keen on hiring me. How can you compete with a stout fellow? And they give me a lower wage compared to others. You work diligently, you are not lazy, and yet, without holding anything back, sometimes you will do more and work better than those who are stout, but everything you get from the boss is the same old tune: you are not strong enough to work well, he says. And since the payment is small, it never comes to anything, I can barely earn enough to buy food and can't bring anything home. If it weren't for my wife working, you would still be walking around barefoot and naked, and would freeze to death in the winter.

"You need, my son, to cook up something," his mother said. "Look at people and consult with them about where you can go, where it would be better to earn money. Might you ask Lyskotun: what doesn't he know? He knows everything. He's seen a bit of the world. And how much he has earned! Look at his mother, she used to be poorer than me, and now she's dressed like a city-dweller. Or look at him: when he dresses up for a holiday and goes out into the street, he could easily pass for our scribe. And does he bring home money and all sorts of good things? Ask him, my son, where you should go. Or maybe you should you go together with him!"

"I asked him, mother, I begged him to take me with him. We will, I say, work together. As you work, so will I. I will not lag behind you.

"And what did he say?"

"But! When he heard this, his eyes bugged out at me. They were glaring, and he himself turned crimson. He looked at me for a long time, and then straining was able to say: "How do you make money? Work like I do," he says, "and you will become rich. I don't need company, look for somebody else to tag along with." And he moved quickly away from me. But after that, as soon as I try to chat with him, he moves away from me. And when we are together, he looks me straight in the eye and continues to stare at me. I move toward him, and he moves right away from me. I will give him a break! He is rich, and prideful compared to me, a poor man. I don't want to bother him. I'll do things on my own. And what, mom, do I think I should still go to the province, will things not be more fortunate for me there?"

"Oh, my son, my darling, isn't it too far? As much as a hundred and fifty versts[28]. To whom will you leave us? But how can you go such a distance alone? It's as though it's at the end of the world!"

"Momma, what shall we do? I will go for the last time. If there is no good fortune there, I will not go anywhere. It will be as it will be. A rolling stone gathers no moss."

His mother was worried. His wife was crying profusely, but there was nothing else to do – they had to see Trokhym off to the province. They heard that there was a fair on the Feast of the Immaculate Virgin, and sometimes a great one, one to which merchants from all over would come, and all kinds of goods were brought, and they heard that people could earn a lot of money there, depending on their luck.

Our Trokhym reached the province. He inquired where the fair was. So many people, so many people! You can't make your way through them! He also steered his way between the people, but he himself did not know where and why. He wondered if he could find a place where his comrades were looking for work. Suddenly someone grabbed his arm and said:

"My fellow townsman! What, you are looking for a job, aren't you?"

Trokhym looked, and it was a merchant, the one who had shaved his beard and walked like a gentleman. He quickly took off his hat, bowed down, and said:

....

[28] A verst is 3500 feet or a little longer than a kilometer.

"We ask, gentleman merchant, whether God will send a good master."

"Are you an honest man and not a slacker? Not a lazy man?"

"Since I was born, I haven't done anything bad. I don't even have any such thoughts. I will work and you will see for yourself."

"Follow me then."

So, he brought Trokhym to his quarters. And all the lorries were standing there, with stacked cases, boxes, everything with goods, and everything packed. The shopkeeper ordered: "When the drivers come with the horses, let them harness them and then transport everything to my shop. They already know where it is. You remain with them and move all the boxes to my shop, and do not leave sight of the goods. Here is your comrade."

Trokhym glanced at his comrade, and it was Denys Lyskotun, only no longer as smartly dressed as he had been in his village. His clothes were old, and there was no sign of a belt, and his hat was quite shabby.

"Hello, my brother Denys!" Trokhym said to him immediately.

"How come you are here?"

"How come! After all, you have not been here in your life, but you have come, and I come here often."

They exchanged words. Trokhym asked about what he could earn, the wages for a day's work, and other details about the job, but Denys did not seem to want to talk to him, said a word as if he hadn't eaten, and turns away from him.

"As I see him," Trokhym thought to himself, "he is much more prideful than he was in our village: but, you see, he pretends to be poor in order to earn a higher wage. He's damn cunning!"

The merchant rejoiced that both his workmen were from the same village and were friends and told them all the work that needed to be done and went away. He did not say what he would pay Trokhym, by the day or weekly.

Trokhym became concerned and asked Denys what to do.

"Damn him and his mother!" If he doesn't pay like we think he should, then we will reward ourselves. Hold fast to me, and listen, so that we will eat bread forever."

Trokhym was a little surprised, hearing such a thing from Denys, despite his fame. And he thought to himself, "What is this he is saying? Who knows!" and he began to inspect the lorries filled with goods.

Here the drivers came with the horses, harnessed them, and carted the goods to the shop. Then they unloaded them out and put them away. And then the shop owner came, paid the drivers, let them go, closed the shop, and began to take the lids off the cases, and to take out the goods. Merciful Lord! It was all silver and gold. There was nothing at all made of wood or bone. It was all silver and gold, silver and gold! Spoons, and plates, and knives, and forks. There were also all sorts of cups, made for lords and ladies, and all kinds of goods. There were also many religious things, all of them were made of silver and gold. So many snuff boxes, and earrings, and rings, you could set out sacks of them!

Workers unpacked the things and handed them to the shop-owner, and he unwrapped everything and set it out... Trokhym was afraid to look at the goods, seeing how valuable they were. And Denys did not seem to care much. He would pick something and weigh it on his hand, as if he knew a lot about it.

The shop owner gave orders to Denys more than he did to Trokhym, because the former was quicker to understand and more agile, and it was clear that he was not doing such things for the first time and has dealt with this before. And Trokhym was in the province and at such an elegant fair for the first time, and for the first time he saw such goods that he had never dreamt of. So, he was puzzled, and did not know how to do anything. So, he seemed to be slow and somewhat thick.

The shop owner taught Denys how to lock the shop with German locks. They are so tricky! And they unlock backward and come apart in three parts, and who knows how they are made. If you don't know how to, you can't unlock them, so then you can't lock them. The shop owner locked the locks, gave the two men each a fifty-kopeck piece, and told them to have a good time wherever they wanted to go, and in the evening to come to his quarters for supper.

Our compatriots went everywhere at the fair. So what? Denys's buddies came to him immediately, all the Russkys, who were probably his old acquaintances: they greeted him, and asked where he had been, and then began to whisper, to look at Trokhym, and to say something about him. He felt terrified, and he skirted away from them. He went to the bazaar, bought bread, cucumbers, wheat, and melon. He came to the quarters, had a good lunch, and lay down, waiting for the shopkeeper. It was not soon after that Denys came, and it was evident that there was a little something on his mind, and he went to bed quickly. And he didn't want to have supper, saying that his head hurt.

The shop-owner came and gave Trokhym a glass of vodka and supper. And what a good dish it was! Borscht with beef, buckwheat groats with pig lard, also baked meat, a quarter leg of lamb. After all, the shop owner said to him:

"You'll be paid and fed like that every day through the fair, just serve me honestly. Tomorrow early in the morning go to the shop. My attendants will come out, whatever they say, obey them as you would me. Take care while sitting by the shop so that no one steals anything. At night you will take turns with Denys and walk with the watchmen near the shop, one of you until midnight, and the other from then till dawn. If you notice anything or see something wrong with my shop, tell me right away. Wake me up even at midnight.

In addition to your daily wage, I will reward you for your sincerity if you are honest."

From the bottom of his heart, Trokhym, going to bed, prayed to God and thanked Him for his mercy, that he had delivered him such work. There is no need to feed himself, the food is good, of a kind that he doesn't have at home even at Eastertime, and fifty more kopecks every day! Ten days of the fair – ten fifty kopeck pieces, and I'll bring five rubles home. Glory to you, O Lord! And here he promised to serve sincerely and secure the merchant's goods better than his own.

The fair began. The merchants, having laid out their goods, opened their shops. The lords and ladies set off fussing about. They walked around, examined the goods, made estimates, haggled, and bought. Our Trokhym saw enough of the gentlemen.

Looking at them, he carefully looked over the passers-by, so that each would go his own way, and so that he would not look too much at the goods in the shop, because this is already a sign of bad intent in a man. And when it happened that there was a man standing next to the shop and looking here and there, Trokhym – it's a shame to say – would chase him away, because such a man stands there as if it's apparently nothing. And when he saw that the watchmen were looking somewhere else, and the passer-by would come closer, and he himself shuffled farther away. Trokhym more than anything else looked after this; and Denys – did not do a thing because he had no time. Often, as soon as the lords and ladies had gathered at the shop, the Russkys, the Gypsies, and the Jews, all of them would come over to Denys and take him aside, and they whispered and chattered with him for a long time.

Trokhym asked him who they were and why they were coming to him. Then Denys frowned and angrily said: "Why are you looking after somebody else? Keep to your own busi ness. I don't look after you, so don't look after me either. They are my old acquaintances. I worked with them in the city."

And where could they have worked in the mud, that they were all so shabbily dressed and ragged that it was disgusting to look at them!

Once a gypsy woman approached, and she looked truly disgusting, like a really old man. While walking by the shop she winked at Denys. The latter went with her over to the corner, and they whispered something to each other. Trokhym watched them for a long time, and he felt a knot in his stomach, feeling that something was off. After having her fill of talking, the gypsy woman left. Denys sat down and kept sitting for a while and then came over to Trokhym, and after looking at him for a long time, said:

"Your poverty is great, but you don't know how to deal with it. You sincerely serve yourself for your own misfortune. And hardly will the shop owner give you what you deserve to earn."

"How are you going to earn more?" Trokhym asked. "After all, even here the pay is good, and the work is not hard, but you can't earn any more."

"Yes, you can."

"Tell me, how is that?"

"Okay, I will! And tell me, Trokhym, truthfully, are you diligently serving your master?"

"And how else can you serve, if not with all sincerity? It is said: if you hire yourself out, you've sold yourself. I don't want the master's crumbs, and if I should see that my own brother does not think about the master's goods and destroys him, then I would expose my brother."

"Godspeed to you, Trokhym!" Denys said to him and slapped him lightly on his shoulder. "Work forever, and you will get rich!" And he turned away from him, and Trokhym noticed that he, having turned away from him, was smiling.

"What happened to our Denys?" Trokhym thought to himself. "He's different here from what he was in our village."

He sat thinking about it, and again the same gypsy woman walked past the shop, and Denys approached her and said: "Stupid! Don't talk to him. We'll do it ourselves."

Trokhym heard this, and the gypsy woman left.

It was getting dark. The shop attendants began to scatter: some to the theater, some to the bathhouse, some to who knows where... The last one cleaned up the shop, exited, and said to Denys, as happened every evening: "Lock the shop and give me the keys." Denys closed the door, prepared the locks, and turned them: the second one was tight, so much so that it screeched as he pulled and twisted it. He handed over the keys, and the attendant left. For some reason Denys turned away, and Trokhym quietly, furtively touched the locks... "Holy Mother of God! Not even a single one is locked!" All three were hanging open. Denys struggled for a long time to lock them up. "This is what Denys is!"

Just as Trokhym was thinking to himself, Denys said:

"Go, friend, to our quarters, and bring out supper as soon as possible, and go to bed. Or do you know what? It's stuffy there. I'll spend the whole night on guard duty. Don't come after midnight, get a good sleep. I'm still not sleepy all the same. I'll do the guarding all night by myself."

"That's what it means! Wait!" Trokhym thought to himself and walked on quietly, until at first, when he dropped by, Denys already could no longer see him, so there was nothing left to do, so he began to hurry over to his shopkeeper's house. At that time, the master of the house, having called guests over, was offering them tea. Then Trokhym came in and told him everything about how he had noticed Denys being up to something, how everything was being done, and how Denys had seemingly locked the shop and gotten rid of Trokhym.

When the owner heard everything, he was at first so frightened that he turned pale; then he began to thank Trokhym for being so loyal, and offered him two cups of tea, one sweet and the other especially sweet, still thanking him for his frankness and honest soul. And then he hurriedly sent someone to find the attendant with the keys. With difficulty, they found him somewhere. The shopkeeper snatched the keys, lit the lantern, and, getting in a light carriage, hurried over to the shop.

He ran up, looked around, and so it was – not a single lock was locked. He started calling Denys, but there was no sign of him.

Apparently, he was still sitting next to the shop, but when he saw the owner with a lantern, he figured out that there must be a reason, so he hid away here from the spot where he was lurking, waiting to see what would come of this.

The owner bolted into the shop... Glory be to You, Lord! Everything is intact, everything is safe! The thief had not yet begun to fiddle about. Apparently, he was waiting for the dead of midnight. Having already locked all the locks properly, he immediately ordered two of the watchmen to guard his shop all night and returned to his quarters.

And he was already thanking Trokhym! He embraced him for averting such a calamity, and for having told him in advance about such impending disaster. Then he took out a silver ruble coin and gave it to him, saying:

"I'm not going to give you just a fifty-kopeck coin each day, but from today on a whole ruble. I will give you a reward, as I know for myself, for being an honest man. Try hard going forward: what you notice, what you hear, tell me right away! Now don't go to the shop, lest that idler might do something bad to you. There are guards there now."

And when they heard in the morning that as many as three stalls had been robbed, the shop owner thanked Trokhym even more for warning him. "It would have happened to me," he said, "And there, although much was taken, it was not a large sum. And even if they had stolen a little from me, it would still have been tens of thousands."

Trokhym still thought that Denys must have been working with the thieves. "Merciful Lord," he thought, "how quickly that man has become lazy! What a brave fellow he used to be, you can't think of anyone better, but now he has become totally wicked!" After that night he did not see him again.

Once Trokhym was sitting by the stall and looking about: with weapons in hand, the police were leading the arrested, who were both in front of and behind them. Trokhym looked closer, and Denys was walking among them. "What a shame!" Trokhym thought, and he felt sorry for his fellow townsman. He ran up quickly to him and handed him whatever money he had on him for his expenses in prison. How did Denys react? He glanced quickly and when he saw that it was Trokhym, he gnashed his teeth, his eyes glowed, and he cast the alms to the ground. He said: "It would be better for you to be dead than to see me in such disgrace!" He walked away without looking back.

Trokhym related this to the owner, and the latter said, "They've caught all those who were stealing from the stalls, and they've arrested our Denys, too. He is accused of being with them, of bringing them to my stall, but he won't confess to anything."

The fair came to an end. Everyone settled their accounts, and the owner settled with Trokhym as well. Every day he would give him a silver coin, but this time he bid farewell and handed him a hundred rubles, saying, "Take it, dear Trokhym! You've saved me tens of thousands. I thank you."

Trokhym was overjoyed! And why wouldn't he be? How much money he was bringing home! He had never earned so much before! Thankful that the owner had given him gold coins, he thought to hide them in such a way that he wouldn't lose them, so that no one would notice he had them.

He would keep silver coins in a different place. He decided to stitch the gold coins in his footwraps, while the silver coins, rubles, half-rubles, and smaller change he sewed into the lining of his coat. In this way, it was impossible to tell that he had money on him.

Having gathered his belongings, he set off from the province, heading straight home. "Why go to other places when I've done well enough?" he thought on his way. "Thank God, I've earned a lot, and we'll all benefit from this. I'll buy a horse, fix up the wagon – it's a better source of income than when you are forced to walk. I'll buy flax for my wife to spin. She can hire someone to help her, and they'll both earn more. I'll provide my mother with everything she desires. May she live in comfort in her old age, after all the hardships she's endured. I'll clothe the children, gather firewood for winter, buy everything we need, and we'll live without any worries," he thought.

With a light heart, he continued his journey, eager to bring joy to his family, as God had granted him good fortune. He had just over fifty versts left to reach his village when suddenly, he spotted someone catching up with him. Who was it? It was Denys! When Trokhym saw him, his limbs went weak; his stomach churned; his heart raced; and he felt a sense of foreboding. There was no way to avoid him. They were on the same road. He would be happy to walk faster to reach the village before Denys caught up. In the village, he could wait and hide until Denys went far away. But Trokhym was exhausted after covering so much distance. No matter how hard he would try, Denys would overtake him easily, as the latter was stronger and more accustomed to walking.

Trokhym saw that there was nothing he could do, so he thought, "Well, it is God's will! I won't walk with him. I'll keep my distance. I'll tarry, and he'll eventually move past me."

He walked on, and then Denys caught up to him. Denys tapped him on the shoulder and said, "Hello, friend! Are you trying to run away from me?"

"Hello, Denys! Where did you come from?" Trokhym asked.

"Did you think Denys has already become a lazy bum, that he'd go to a labor camp, and you'd rush home to tell everyone I got caught?"

"God be with you! Why would I do that to you? I felt sorry for you when I saw you in such a predicament."

"You felt sorry for me?"

"Yes, I did. You've never done any harm to me, neither have I to you. So, what's the point? Tell me, how did you manage to get out of that mess?"

Denys gave Trokhym a look that sent shivers down his spine and chilled his soul. Then Denys spoke, "Get out of it? But I was smeared. Don't they smear a man for no reason?"

"Surely, they do. What a relief to know you weren't with them."

"Am I some kind of criminal, huh?" Denys snapped at him.

"Who's thinking that about you? God forbid!" For a while they walked in silence. Eventually, Denys spoke up again, his voice much harsher than before, as if it were not really him talking, "Do you think I disappeared because of those locks?"

"What locks are you talking about?"

"The ones you think I know nothing about?"

"God be with you! I only heard about those locks, and I've already forgotten about them."

"Forgotten! You'll really forget."

And they fell silent again as they continued walking, eventually passing through a small village.

Trokhym had an acquaintance in the area and wanted to take a break. "No need for that!" Denys shouted at him, and poor Trokhym obeyed, fearing that since Denys was three times as strong as he was. He might cause trouble. Trokhym reckoned, "I won't provoke him. I'll just comply and let him boss me around until I reach my own place, and then I'll get away from him."

After passing through the village, Denys turned off the road and into a small grove, calling Trokhym to follow him.

"We'll rest here," Denys said as he sat down under a pear tree. "Let's see if you have anything to eat, and we can have lunch or an afternoon snack."

"What do I have?" Trokhym replied, taking some bread from his bag, dry fish, and a few cucumbers.

Denys pulled out a menacing-looking knife from his bootleg. Trokhym froze when he saw it. Denys acted as if he were in charge and cut some bread for himself first, then handed a piece to Trokhym. He also took the best pieces of dry fish and threw a few cucumbers to Trokhym as if he were tossing a bone to a dog. Trokhym endured all this in silence, thinking, "Just get me home, Lord. Keep him away from me. I want nothing to do with him."

"You know what, buddy?" Denys said after getting his fill of eating, "To hell with walking during the day! Let's rest during the day; it's so hot! We'll cover more ground at night and continue further with the coolness of that time and the starlight. After resting today, we'll set off tonight. By the day after tomorrow, we'll be back home. Lie down and take a nap until evening."

The two men lay down and slept soundly. They woke up before sunset, ate Trokhym's food, and continued their way.

"It seems like you don't have anything for the journey," Trokhym remarked.

"Where the hell would I get anything?!" Denys replied. "Whatever I had earned, I spent it all in that damn prison cell. And you'd have had your share, too. You wouldn't have to worry about anything."

"You surprise me, Denys. Were you always like this in our village? It seems like you've become quite daring, traveling all over the place."

"Hush, be quiet; it's none of your business!" Denys snapped, and they fell silent as they continued walking.

After some time had passed, Denys spoke up again, "Hey, friend! First, you'll tell your wife everything, won't you? And then you'll go to the village head, and you'll be going around telling everyone how Denys Lyskotun wanted to steal from the bazaar stall, and how you warned the owner, and how the guards took Denys from the prison for questioning?"

"No, Denys, you don't know me. It's a terrible thing to talk about someone like that. May God forgive you for all your actions, and may you repent and abandon such evil deeds. You stumbled, but now you are ashamed of it. It's not my place to talk about it. Not only won't I tell anything to my wife, but I'm also asking God to help me forget because, I do believe that you will repent."

"Oh, really? Sure thing I'll repent. I'll start ordering morning church services. Money is tight. I haven't earned any. Maybe you'll give me some. Tell me, Trokhym, how much did the shop keeper give you for telling him about the locks?"

"I didn't tell him. He found out on his own."

"Whatever you say, but did he give you anything as a reward?"

"He gave me a reward before letting me go, a few rubles."

"You've earned them all. And how much?"

"Who knows!" Trokhym replied nervously, trembling with fear. It was night, and it was just the two of them, with Denys the stronger of the two. "I really don't know. I didn't count it. I just took it and left."

"It's probably a lot, so much that you couldn't even count it. Will you share it with me?"

"Why should I?"

"To share it like they usually do, half and half. Or maybe you will give it all to me. What a great guy you would be if you gave it all to me."

"What are you saying, Denys?" Trokhym barely managed to speak, realizing how far things were going.

"Ah, to hell with your money then! You must have really a lot if you've gotten so scared. Are you going to tell everyone that I planned to rob you on the way?"

"Please, Denys, don't think like that about me! I told you I wouldn't tell anyone, and I swear on everything, I won't say a word."

"Alright, then swear it!"

Trokhym started swearing to it so earnestly that it was frightening to listen to.

"Now, take an oath!" Denys said, handing him a handful of dirt. "Eat all of this!"

Trokhym, with a sincere heart, having no fear and determined not to tell anyone anything, ate the handful of dirt, swallowing it bit by bit.

"Now, my friend, we're both sure."

That's how Denys had always treated Trokhym. There had always been something to find fault with. Trokhym, being the weaker one, gave in to everything, fearing that Denys might harm him.

They continued walking through the night, and as morning approached, the sun started to rise and shine brightly. They went into a grove to take some rest.

It became scorching hot, with no breeze and no shade. The sun was relentless, making it difficult to breathe. Although the two men tried to sleep, they couldn't find a comfortable spot. The sun was unbearable, and there was no respite from it. At the edge of the forest, the sun was directly overhead, scorching them. They moved deep into the thicket, but it was even worse there. With no relief from the heat, there was just the burning sun pounding down from above, and the slight wind was unable to reach them. They found water, but they couldn't drink enough of it to quench their thirst. Breathing was becoming increasingly difficult. They dug small pits for themselves, lying down to find a bit of relief. They warmed up and moved to another spot. They became so exhausted that they couldn't even move.

The entire day had been cloudless and scorching hot. As the evening approached, the intense heat finally subsided a bit. Our two companions got up, breathed more freely, had something to eat, and then continued on their way.

"If we do our best," Trokhym said, "we'll reach home at sunrise. It's only twenty versts from this forest to our village."

"That's true," Denys replied, "as long as you keep up. Don't lag behind. You're always slowing down. Hurry!"

So, they continued their way, and by the time they had covered seven versts from midday, a black wall of a cloud appeared on the horizon. Thick, golden-ringed clouds started to separate from it like coils. They twisted together and gathered into a wall that kept rising. The sun hid behind the clouds early, and the birds gathered, waiting for something. The male birds called the females and rushed toward them. Those that had chicks went to them, while those that were out sauntering flew off to hide. Everything gradually became still. Not a blade of grass moved. Everything was expecting something big and dreadful.

Then, in the distance, a rumbling started, like the roaring sea or a powerful wind from afar, or the heavy footsteps of many people approaching on horseback, making the ground shake even from a distance. Only lightning was flashing, and the sun disappeared completely. The clouds descended, and nothing could be seen anymore.

"What shall we do?" Denys began to ask. "How shall we go? It will be completely dark soon. It's frightening to walk without seeing the road."

"Look, there's a small grove," Trokhym said. "Let's hurry there."

"Where's the grove? I still can't see anything."

"When the lightning flashes, it's to the right of the road. Let's hurry. It's getting darker."

They rushed forward. The wall had risen, and it was getting very dark. Without the lightning, they couldn't see anything in front of them. The wall was dense, black, and ominous, extending from east to west, and the lightning constantly flickered from every direction. Thunder rumbled with reverberations, as if massive rocks were rolling down a mountain, and then something would crash and fall silent. But then there was a resounding roar that reverberated across the entire sky and every corner of the massive cloud. The thunder would quiet down, but you could hear something humming, rumbling, and seething, even more frightening than the thunder itself. And the lightning was relentless. Every time it flashed they couldn't see anything after it.

"Where are you, Trokhym?" Denys said trembling. "Take my hand and lead me. I can't walk properly. My legs are dragging."

"Hold on to me," Trokhym said. "We're almost there. Look, you can see when the lightning flashes now."

"I'm afraid of this lightning. Oh, if we could get to the forest faster! Look how close the storm is! Here comes the rain... Oh, hurry, hurry!"

Denys leaned heavily on Trokhym's arms, and Trokhym, exhausted, dragged him along. He mustered all his strength to drag Denys under a dense tree and lay him down, then collapsed himself.

The massive storm cloud had now covered the entire sky, turning it into a black canvas. No matter how much you strained your eyes, you couldn't see anything in front of you. The terrible storm raged, making a roaring sound under the heavens. It swept across the fields, pushed against the forest as if it wanted to shove it away and crush it completely. Branches cracked, snapped, and fell. There was something terrible roaring there. It whistled throughout the entire forest. Thunder covered everything... and then suddenly, boom! Something fell; the earth shook. And then the thunder roared again, and again the earth shook. And again, there was the same whistling and clamor, and again, something fell and cracked! It was the storm raging. Ancient oaks fell like twigs! When the rain poured, it didn't just rain, it poured. It rumbled through the forest, rushed down from the mountains in streams, and gurgled... and from it, from the raging storm, and from the thunder that tore through the skies, there was such a clamor and roaring that it's frightening even to recall! And here, lightning blinded with its red fiery glow... It was like doomsday!

Denys couldn't lie down, couldn't sit still, and couldn't stand in one place. He walked, darting from under one tree to another, wringing his hands, not knowing what to do with himself. "Trokhym, Trokhym! Are you asleep? Aren't you afraid of anything?" he said loudly, trembling with fear.

"No, I'm not asleep, and I'm not afraid of anything."

"What if the lightning strikes?"

"It's God's will! I know that, and even though I'm lying down, I'm praying to God."

"Will He have mercy on me if I pray to Him? Oh! How it cracked in the woods again!"

"He will, just repent...."

"How can such a sinner like me repent? How can God forgive me?"

"Why not! Repent sincerely. Your sins aren't that great. You're as sinful as any other per... Lord! What's that?"

At this point, they both fell to the ground... A fiery arrow cut through the entire sky, and in the blink of an eye, it struck the same tree that Denys had been standing under, and he came up to Trokhym. The tree was incredibly tall. It was split into splinters up to its midpoint, and all its branches were crushed and flattened, leaving no trace of them. Denys barely managed to get to his feet, but the distance between them and the tree where they had been standing was only about ten sazhens[29]. After regaining his composure a bit, Denys grabbed Trokhym's hands and began pleading: "Let's go, let's go from here! God will strike us here."

"Where can we hide?" Trokhym asked him. "Can't you see how bad it is everywhere in the forest? Look, the lightning struck the tree. It's on fire. And it's not far from us, and there's havoc in the whole forest."

"Oh, it's terrifying, terrifying! Who is sitting and watching over me?"

"God is with you! There's no one. Pray to God instead!"

"God won't spare me. Do you think I'm... Oh, my face is burning!"

"He will spare you, I'm telling you. Pray and repent."

"Who am I to repent? I'm the one who robbed you all. There wasn't any other thief in the village... it's my doing. I was acting on a tip from others... I robbed all of you... handed things over to the gypsies and Russky soldiers... I took the money and got richer... I robbed the shops... and got away with it! I wanted to do to you what I did to that one who is sitting and glaring at me...," Denys said, not understanding anything he was saying, and beating his chest with his fists.

Then suddenly, as lightning flashed around them and thunder roared as if the sky was falling on them, both fell unconscious. Trokhym, soaked by the rain, gradually regained his senses. He saw Denys running around him, wringing his hands, as pale as death, and shouting, "I'm not just a thief. I'm a murderer! I killed that poor man. I was supposed to find money on him. My clothes are stained with blood, and he's accusing me... Oh Lord! And won't you forgive me?"

Denys began to run around as if he had lost his mind. Trokhym, managing to get to his feet, tried to calm him down and bring him to his senses.

....

[29] A unit of measurement equivalent to about seven feet.

"No," Denys cried, "God will punish me. The thunder will strike me down. I'm a thief! I pretended to be good, blamed others, and I was going to kill you so that you wouldn't tell anyone in the village about the stall at the bazaar... Now tell everyone who I really am! God is about to kill me! Tell everyone how wicked I am."

"God is with you, Denys!" Trokhym said. "What are you thinking? Believe me and God Almighty that, as I have sworn, I will not betray you. I will keep my word, and I will not condemn you for anything."

Trokhym tried to comfort him while the thunder rumbled on, and the lightning burned their eyes. Every time the thunder struck, trees cracked and branches fell. Denys in his insanity continued his confession, admitting to being a murderer and a thief, pretending to be good and so on. Then he hallucinated an old man, scolding him, and out of his mind Denys began to recount how he had killed him. He pleaded with Trokhym to tell everyone about his crimes, so that they would avoid him.

The thunder roared and rattled, but then it started to subside as the storm clouds moved away. The rain also calmed down, and the lightning, which had been blinding, gradually diminished. Trokhym looked around and saw that sunrise was approaching.

"Let's go, Denys,'" he said. "We're not far from our village now. Let's move quickly."

"Trokhym, dear friend!" Denys said, without moving from his spot. "I'm afraid to move. I feel like thunder is all around me, and I can still see that accursed old man. Trokhym, my dear friend! Don't tell anyone anything.'"

"And Trokhym had to reassure Denys again. One way or another, they continued.

Whether in the predawn hours or with the sun already risen, they hurried along. The entire way Denys, lost in thought, couldn't utter a word. But then he shouted:

"I'd be better off if lightning had struck me!"

"God knows what you're thinking," Trokhym said, glancing at Denys and becoming alarmed. Denys's eyes were burning like fire, and he seemed to be in a wild frenzy. But Trokhym continued to reassure him:

"Cheer up," he said, "we're only five versts away; we're almost in our field."

"Only five versts! But what if we meet someone along the way, and you betray me? You'd be better off dead!" with these words, Denys pushed Trokhym to the ground and sat on top of him.

"What are you doing, Denys," Trokhym moaned beneath Denys and then began to beg: "Let me go, brother, my dear friend, my falcon! I swear by all that is holy, I won't tell anyone anything! Take all the money I have here, just don't destroy your soul and mine! Spare my poor children, don't take away my wife's husband. Who will take care of my aged mother? I will treat you like my dear father all my life! Don't let me die without a confession! Please, give me just a little time to pray to God...."

"You'll pray in heaven!" Denys replied, furious as a beast, while he held Trokhym's arms down with one hand and pressed his knee against his chest. He took a knife out of the top of his boot. No matter how quickly he tried, he couldn't deal with the poor victim with just one hand... And Trokhym kept pleading, finally whispering, "Dear God!... May God provide a witness to my innocent death!"

Then the wind began to roll tumbleweed toward them, closer and closer. Trokhym looked at it plaintively and said, "Let this tumbleweed be a witness that you are ending my life unjustly!"

"Let it witness as much as it wants! You couldn't have found a better witness," Denys said, as he chuckled and unsheathed the knife with his teeth. That was the knife he had used to cut Trokhym's bread that had nourished him throughout their journey.

"Oh, merciful Lord! Take my soul! My wife, my children, my father...." Denys prepared to strike with his knife. Laughing, he still wanted to say something. But a guardian angel, to prevent Denys from making any more sarcastic remarks, splashed the victim's blood right into his mouth, taking the righteous, innocent man's soul and carrying it straight to heaven.

Two shepherds, frightened and trembling, abandoned their herd and ran to the village head. They reported that a man had been found murdered in a certain place. They couldn't identify the victim, as they were too frightened to get a good look. The village head immediately dispatched the appropriate authorities to watch over the body and instructed them not to go closer to it themselves and not to let anyone approach it. Anyone who interfered or did anything suspicious would be taken into custody.

Immediately, a report was sent to the district court about the case of the "suddenly deceased, unidentified man who had been stabbed to death, who was lying peacefully at the very spot where his death occurred."

Some of the villagers had gone to find work elsewhere and hadn't returned yet, but their wives were unconcerned. Trokhym's wife and mother, upon hearing the news, shouted in unison, "Oh, dear Lord! It must be Trokhym! It has to be him!" Their hearts felt it.

They begged the village head to allow them to go and see if it was Trokhym – to wash his body well, and, if possible, bring him home. That was the task of women, but they did not understand the law. The village head, not allowing anyone to approach the body, sternly forbade it and ordered them to wait until the investigator arrived and cleared the way.

On the following day, Denys appeared in the village. He was dressed even better than before. He was cheerful, talkative, and joking with everyone he met. He saw that people were gathering at the local administration office, so he headed there. They informed him that they had found a murdered man, and Denys, unable to contain himself, asked:

"What are his wife and mother saying?"

"Whose?" the village head replied in surprise.

"Well, you... or whoever said it! They say it's Trokhym!"

"It's still not clear, and none of us have even thought about that, let alone said anything. Many men had left the village for work. Maybe he's not one of ours."

"Whoever he is, let him lie there until we identify him," Denys said with a laugh. "And witnesses will reveal whoever committed the murder."

Some young men present burst into laughter and said, "Oh, to hell with Denys! He would always have something witty to say. Where can we find witnesses out in an open field? When he got into a fight, it was man against man...."

Then the bell rang. The investigator himself ran up and immediately shouted, "Where is the dead body?"

"At the scene, Your Honor!" the village head replied.

"Scribe, take some honest people as witnesses, have them take an oath, and lead them to the body. I'll be there shortly. Village head, come with me!" Inside the house, the investigator locked the door and questioned the village head, asking if he suspected anyone and if anyone had said anything about the matter. Since the village head considered Denys an honest man, he didn't mention the latter's earlier slip of the tongue or report it. The matter was left at that. The doctor arrived and the witnesses took an oath. The investigator noticed Denys among them and asked, "Why did you take this young man as a witness? We need honest elders for this."

"This man, Your Honor," the village head replied, "even though he is young, we don't have any elders with such intelligence, wisdom, and acumen. He can analyze everything intelligently."

The village head whispered this to the investigator while glancing at Denys, who noticed it. When the investigator heard it from the village head, he also looked at Denys and said loudly, "Very well, bring him here!"

Upon hearing this, Denys turned pale, and the investigator took note, though he didn't say anything.

They all gathered at the location where the body lay. The investigator ordered the witnesses to testify if there were any signs of struggle.

"There are none!" Denys shouted from a distance. "Why would there be? Just one stab with a knife, that's all."

The investigator noticed this and remained silent.

During the examination, they found that the lining of the coat had been cut apart, and when they found a small silver coin nearby, they suspected that there had been money in the coat that had been taken. Upon removing the boots and footwraps they found five gold coins stitched inside. Denys lost control of himself and exclaimed, "See, he didn't confess!" But after saying this, he came to his senses, looked around, and noticed the investigator scrutinizing him. He didn't know where to look, blinked, turned pale, and quickly moved away to get lost in the crowd. The investigator still didn't say a word.

As Trokhym's wife and mother, followed by his six-year-old son, approached, the wife recognized her husband from a distance and cried out, "Trokhym, Trokhym, my dear Trokhym!" She fell to his side along with his mother, and the young boy, being a child, cried while he crawled around him, and kept looking....

The investigator was about to order them to be taken away so they wouldn't interfere with the proceedings. But instead, he said, "Let them mourn and weep over him. Blood is thicker than water. We will handle our business afterward."

He stood beside them with the doctor, and Denys, who was accustomed to boasting that he was ahead of everyone and equal to the gentry, positioned himself next to the investigator.

They wept and lamented over Trokhym with so much sorrow. His mother said as she cried, "Why did you leave me, my son, my little swan, when you went off to look for work? Who will take care of me, an old and weak woman? It would have been better if death had taken me," she continued. His wife pleaded, "My dear Trokhym, say just one word! Give me counsel: how will the children and I live without you? Say a word, tell me who it is who made us part. Show me if there were any witnesses to your torment. How did you surrender your soul to God?"

"And what is this, Momma?" the little boy shouted, playing with something he had taken from his father's hand.

Upon hearing this, the investigator, with his hat well-shaped and puffed up, said to Denys, who was standing nearby, "Go, see what that is and bring it here."

Denys walked over, examined it, shuddered noticeably, cradled it in his hand, and then threw it away. He himself turned as pale as a white wall.

"Why did you throw it?" the investigator shouted at him. "What is it? Bring it here!"

"Oh, it's nothing, Your Honor, just... a weed," Denys replied, shivering as if he were feverish.

"What kind of weed? Bring it here!"

"Just a weed, some grass. Perhaps, when the deceased was dying, he grabbed onto it, and it remained in his hand."

"What kind of grass is it? Bring it here!" the investigator continued to question, realizing that Denys was becoming increasingly flustered for no apparent reason.

"It's just... a... tumble... weed," Denys barely managed to say.

At this point, the boy picked up one of the many tumbleweeds that had rolled over to there, and he showed it to Denys, saying, "Look, sir, there's more of this! There are many of them lying around Dad. They probably saw everything...."

"You're lying!" Denys shouted, pushing the boy away from him without knowing what to say anymore. His wits had abandoned him, and his tongue had become tangled....

"Enough!" the investigator shouted. "Now tell the whole truth. You knew there were no signs of a struggle on the dead man. You regretted that he didn't confess about the gold coins, and now you're afraid of the tumbleweed. Tell us, why are you afraid of it? Tell us how everything happened."

Denys kept stumbling over his words, and every time he tried to conjure up lies, the investigator interrupted him. Whenever Denys pointed to the tumbleweed, he became so flustered that he couldn't continue. He reluctantly recounted the entire incident, from why he killed Trokhym to how the distraught man pledged the tumbleweed to be his witness. And as he fled from there to wash away the blood, the tumbleweed clung to his legs everywhere in the field. If it weren't for the tumbleweed that the boy had brought, he might have continued to lie.

"That's what a good-for-nothing he is," the investigator said, and then turned to the village head, saying, "How could you appoint such an idler to assist in the investigation?"

"Well, Your Honor," the village head began, followed by all the older and honest elders. "He's an honest man. He never harmed anyone. If everyone in our village were like him, things would be better!"

"Have there been any problems in your village recently? Do you suspect anyone?" the investigator asked.

"Well?" the villagers replied. "There have been occasional problems, but it wasn't him. When we had thefts, he was the one who sometimes found stolen items."

"Speak up, confess! Is this your doing?" the investigator shouted at Denys.

Shaking all over, Denys immediately confessed to everything, from when he began stealing chickens, and realizing that money was plentiful, he continued to commit more crimes. He admitted to having dealings with the Russky soldiers, who engaged in large-scale businesses and stole from everyone. He even had dealings with Gypsies, who were born thieves, and he robbed people with them. He disclosed it all, including how he had killed the frail old man, hoping to find some money to live off. He revealed everything, and how he had framed others as well.

The people, as they listened to him, were horrified, some even slapping their coat flaps, saying, "Who could have trusted him? We thought there wasn't a more clever, industrious, and honest person in the village, and here he turns out to be like this! The main thief, swindler, and murderer!"

"Even if people don't know and think well of someone, if they're idle and try to hide their actions, God will eventually reveal them," the investigator said and ordered Denys to be taken to the city.

Denys Lyskotun received his just punishment for all his deeds. He got his just desserts. The executioner gave Denys a good thrashing, and he was sent to labor camps in a desolate land of no return.

Indeed, divine justice does not tolerate injustice, and even though the ends are hidden, God reveals them. And through what kind of a little thing? A weed, a simple tumbleweed.

Kharkiv

ABOUT THE AUTHOR

Hryhoriy Kvitka-Osnovyanenko (1778–1843) is considered by many to be "the father of Ukrainian prose" and deserving of a wider readership. Born to a prominent Ukrainian family from just outside of Kharkiv, he became a tireless cultural activist for his Ukrainian people. His prose works such as the sentimentalist *Marusya* (1833) and the comic *The Witch of Konotop* (1837) along with his theatrical works such as *Matchmaking at Honcharivka* (1834) earn him a place in the pantheon of nineteenth-century Ukrainian writers.

ABOUT THE TRANSLATORS

Michael Naydan is Woskob Family Professor of Ukrainian Studies at The Pennsylvania State University. He has published over 50 articles on literary topics and more than 80 translations in journals and anthologies. He has translated, co-translated, or edited more than 40 books of translations, including Mark Andryczyk's *Ukraine 22: Ukrainian Writers Respond to War* (Penguin Books, 2023), *Zelensky: A Biography* (Polity Press, 2023), Yuri Vynnychuk's *The Night Reporter: A 1938 Lviv Murder Mystery* (Glagoslav Publications, 2021), *Selected Poetry of Bohdan Rubchak: Songs of Love, Songs of Death, Songs of the Moon* (Glagoslav Publications, 2020); Maria Matios's novel *Sweet Darusya: A Tale of Two Villages* and Yuri Vynnychuk's novel of the Shoah *Tango of Death* (both with Spuyten Duyvil Publishers, 2019). His own novel about the city of Lviv *Seven Signs of the Lion* appeared with Glagoslav Publications in 2016. He has co-translated several of these and other volumes with Alla Perminova. He has received numerous prizes for his translations including the George S.N. Luckyj Award in Ukrainian Literature Translation from the Canadian Foundation for Ukrainian Studies in 2013.

Alla Perminova is a professor of English at the Autonomous University of Barcelona and a practicing literary translator from and into Ukrainian, English, and Spanish. She received her doctoral and postdoctoral degrees in translation studies from Taras Shevchenko National University of Kyiv where she worked as a full professor for fifteen years. She is

Oleh Olzhych National Literary Contest first prize winner (1997), Fulbright senior scholar (The Pennsylvania State University, 2012–2013), the author of 70 scholarly articles, translator and/or editor of 20 books, presenter of over 30 talks at international conferences. Her personal philosophy as a translator and a researcher is discussed in her book *A Translator's Reception of Contemporary American Poetry* (in Ukrainian, 2015), in which she promotes the reception model of literary translation.

Glagoslav Publications Catalogue

- *The Time of Women* by Elena Chizhova
- *Andrei Tarkovsky: A Life on the Cross* by Lyudmila Boyadzhieva
- *Sin* by Zakhar Prilepin
- *Hardly Ever Otherwise* by Maria Matios
- *Khatyn* by Ales Adamovich
- *The Lost Button* by Irene Rozdobudko
- *Christened with Crosses* by Eduard Kochergin
- *The Vital Needs of the Dead* by Igor Sakhnovsky
- *The Sarabande of Sara's Band* by Larysa Denysenko
- *A Poet and Bin Laden* by Hamid Ismailov
- *Zo Gaat Dat in Rusland* (Dutch Edition) by Maria Konjoekova
- *Kobzar* by Taras Shevchenko
- *The Stone Bridge* by Alexander Terekhov
- *Moryak* by Lee Mandel
- *King Stakh's Wild Hunt* by Uladzimir Karatkevich
- *The Hawks of Peace* by Dmitry Rogozin
- *Harlequin's Costume* by Leonid Yuzefovich
- *Depeche Mode* by Serhii Zhadan
- *Groot Slem en Andere Verhalen* (Dutch Edition) by Leonid Andrejev
- *METRO 2033* (Dutch Edition) by Dmitry Glukhovsky
- *METRO 2034* (Dutch Edition) by Dmitry Glukhovsky
- *A Russian Story* by Eugenia Kononenko
- *Herstories, An Anthology of New Ukrainian Women Prose Writers*
- *The Battle of the Sexes Russian Style* by Nadezhda Ptushkina
- *A Book Without Photographs* by Sergey Shargunov
- *Down Among The Fishes* by Natalka Babina
- *disUNITY* by Anatoly Kudryavitsky
- *Sankya* by Zakhar Prilepin
- *Wolf Messing* by Tatiana Lungin
- *Good Stalin* by Victor Erofeyev
- *Solar Plexus* by Rustam Ibragimbekov
- *Don't Call me a Victim!* by Dina Yafasova
- *Poetin* (Dutch Edition) by Chris Hutchins and Alexander Korobko

- *A History of Belarus* by Lubov Bazan
- *Children's Fashion of the Russian Empire* by Alexander Vasiliev
- *Empire of Corruption: The Russian National Pastime* by Vladimir Soloviev
- *Heroes of the 90s: People and Money. The Modern History of Russian Capitalism* by Alexander Solovev, Vladislav Dorofeev and Valeria Bashkirova
- *Fifty Highlights from the Russian Literature* (Dutch Edition) by Maarten Tengbergen
- *Bajesvolk* (Dutch Edition) by Michail Chodorkovsky
- *Dagboek van Keizerin Alexandra* (Dutch Edition)
- *Myths about Russia* by Vladimir Medinskiy
- *Boris Yeltsin: The Decade that Shook the World* by Boris Minaev
- *A Man Of Change: A study of the political life of Boris Yeltsin*
- *Sberbank: The Rebirth of Russia's Financial Giant* by Evgeny Karasyuk
- *To Get Ukraine* by Oleksandr Shyshko
- *Asystole* by Oleg Pavlov
- *Gnedich* by Maria Rybakova
- *Marina Tsvetaeva: The Essential Poetry*
- *Multiple Personalities* by Tatyana Shcherbina
- *The Investigator* by Margarita Khemlin
- *The Exile* by Zinaida Tulub
- *Leo Tolstoy: Flight from Paradise* by Pavel Basinsky
- *Moscow in the 1930* by Natalia Gromova
- *Laurus* (Dutch edition) by Evgenij Vodolazkin
- *Prisoner* by Anna Nemzcr
- *The Crime of Chernobyl: The Nuclear Goulag* by Wladimir Tchertkoff
- *Alpine Ballad* by Vasil Bykau
- *The Complete Correspondence of Hryhory Skovoroda*
- *The Tale of Avpi* by Ak Weluupar
- *Selected Poems* by Lydia Grigorieva
- *The Fantastic Worlds of Yuri Vynnychuk*
- *The Garden of Divine Songs and Collected Poetry of Hryhory Skovoroda*
- *Adventures in the Slavic Kitchen: A Book of Essays with Recipes* by Igor Klekh
- *Seven Signs of the Lion* by Michael M. Naydan

- *Forefathers' Eve* by Adam Mickiewicz
- *One-Two* by Igor Eliseev
- *Girls, be Good* by Bojan Babić
- *Time of the Octopus* by Anatoly Kucherena
- *The Grand Harmony* by Bohdan Ihor Antonych
- *The Selected Lyric Poetry Of Maksym Rylsky*
- *The Shining Light* by Galymkair Mutanov
- *The Frontier: 28 Contemporary Ukrainian Poets - An Anthology*
- *Acropolis: The Wawel Plays* by Stanisław Wyspiański
- *Contours of the City* by Attyla Mohylny
- *Conversations Before Silence: The Selected Poetry of Oles Ilchenko*
- *The Secret History of my Sojourn in Russia* by Jaroslav Hašek
- *Mirror Sand: An Anthology of Russian Short Poems*
- *Maybe We're Leaving* by Jan Balaban
- *Death of the Snake Catcher* by Ak Welsapar
- *A Brown Man in Russia* by Vijay Menon
- *Hard Times* by Ostap Vyshnia
- *The Flying Dutchman* by Anatoly Kudryavitsky
- *Nikolai Gumilev's Africa* by Nikolai Gumilev
- *Combustions* by Srđan Srdić
- *The Sonnets* by Adam Mickiewicz
- *Dramatic Works* by Zygmunt Krasiński
- *Four Plays* by Juliusz Słowacki
- *Little Zinnobers* by Elena Chizhova
- *We Are Building Capitalism! Moscow in Transition 1992-1997* by Robert Stephenson
- *The Nuremberg Trials* by Alexander Zvyagintsev
- *The Hemingway Game* by Evgeni Grishkovets
- *A Flame Out at Sea* by Dmitry Novikov
- *Jesus' Cat* by Grig
- *Want a Baby and Other Plays* by Sergei Tretyakov
- *Mikhail Bulgakov: The Life and Times* by Marietta Chudakova
- *Leonardo's Handwriting* by Dina Rubina
- *A Burglar of the Better Sort* by Tytus Czyżewski
- *The Mouseiad and other Mock Epics* by Ignacy Krasicki

- *Ravens before Noah* by Susanna Harutyunyan
- *An English Queen and Stalingrad* by Natalia Kulishenko
- *Point Zero* by Narek Malian
- *Absolute Zero* by Artem Chekh
- *Olanda* by Rafał Wojasiński
- *Robinsons* by Aram Pachyan
- *The Monastery* by Zakhar Prilepin
- *The Selected Poetry of Bohdan Rubchak: Songs of Love, Songs of Death, Songs of the Moon*
- *Mebet* by Alexander Grigorenko
- *The Orchestra* by Vladimir Gonik
- *Everyday Stories* by Mima Mihajlović
- *Slavdom* by Ľudovít Štúr
- *The Code of Civilization* by Vyacheslav Nikonov
- *Where Was the Angel Going?* by Jan Balaban
- *De Zwarte Kip* (Dutch Edition) by Antoni Pogorelski
- *Głosy / Voices* by Jan Polkowski
- *Sergei Tretyakov: A Revolutionary Writer in Stalin's Russia* by Robert Leach
- *Opstand* (Dutch Edition) by Władysław Reymont
- *Dramatic Works* by Cyprian Kamil Norwid
- *Children's First Book of Chess* by Natalie Shevando and Matthew McMillion
- *Precursor* by Vasyl Shevchuk
- *The Vow: A Requiem for the Fifties* by Jiří Kratochvil
- *De Bibliothecaris* (Dutch edition) by Mikhail Jelizarov
- *Subterranean Fire* by Natalka Bilotserkivets
- *Vladimir Vysotsky: Selected Works*
- *Behind the Silk Curtain* by Gulistan Khamzayeva
- *The Village Teacher and Other Stories* by Theodore Odrach
- *Duel* by Borys Antonenko-Davydovych
- *War Poems* by Alexander Korotko
- *Ballads and Romances* by Adam Mickiewicz
- *The Revolt of the Animals* by Wladyslaw Reymont
- *Poems about my Psychiatrist* by Andrzej Kotański
- *Someone Else's Life* by Elena Dolgopyat
- *Selected Works: Poetry, Drama, Prose* by Jan Kochanowski

- *The Riven Heart of Moscow (Sivtsev Vrazhek)* by Mikhail Osorgin
- *Bera and Cucumber* by Alexander Korotko
- *The Big Fellow* by Anastasiia Marsiz
- *Boryslav in Flames* by Ivan Franko
- *The Witch of Konotop* by Hryhoriy Kvitka-Osnovyanenko
- *Liza's Waterfall: The Hidden Story of a Russian Feminist* by Pavel Basinsky
- *Biography of Sergei Prokofiev* by Igor Vishnevetsky
- *Ilget* by Alexander Grigorenko
- *The Food Block* by Alexey Ivanov
- *A City Drawn from Memory* by Elena Chizhova
- *Guide to M. Bulgakov's The Master and Margarita* by Ksenia Atarova and Georgy Lesskis

More to come . . .

GLAGOSLAV PUBLICATIONS
www.glagoslav.com